A DEATH in Church

by

Richard M Mattick

ISBN 978-1-916838-30-7

Printed in Great Britain by
Biddles Books Limited, King's Lynn, Norfolk

Foreword

As Rotary District 1100, District Governor, I am delighted to support this new book written by Richard Mattick during the Covid pandemic. I am sure this will inspire Rotarians and non-Rotarians alike as when I look back to COVID times I do sometimes think, what did I achieve? Certainly nothing as inspirational and imaginative as Richard's book?

It is hard to remember sometimes how Zoom meetings often became the norm as both the only way as well as a good way to communicate with others and keep in touch with friends and loved ones. This method still has its place, but nothing takes the place of an inquiring mind and the ability to communicate with others. This book also demonstrates the ability of the human mind to be creative in challenging times so I applaud this book as an example of this.

As a secondary school teacher for over forty years, Youth and Young People are still my passion so I am delighted that District 1100 Intermediate Age Young Photographer, Alex Milton has produced the cover photos for the book. I hope that other Young People will be inspired to use their own creative talents to develop their own short stories.

Anne Bartholomew
District Governor 2023-2024

This book is dedicated to all those Rotarians past and present, real or imaginary who, when there were no cricket or football matches or even church services to attend, kept me company

Author's Note

It has been said before "that a book can take you anywhere and vice versa." Consequently, during lockdown when I could not go out and do all the things I normally did, I could still read and write. If physically my body was confined to a house in Marlborough Road, my mind could roam free across time and place doing what it wanted. Besides the physical isolation another depressing thing about Covid was hearing about younger people with so much to offer who had died. What was the point of a retired magistrate and teacher being alive? Feeling I must have been spared for some reason, I determined to write books for charity. This is my first venture into fiction, a genre with its own problems, not least that you cannot blame your sources! The book is set in 1953 and the language and views of the characters are reflective of the time. if it was the same as this year, with a Coronation and an Ashes series, many other things were different. All of the characters who speak in this book, with the exception of Raynor Goddard, are fictional but many of the places and cases are real and if they stimulate you to read more about them so much the better. In front of Chapter One is a list of characters. I suggest you skip reading this but refer back to it if you are unsure who somebody is or what their role is. I have tried, probably unsuccessfully to avoid anachronisms but feel free to let me know where I have failed.

So open the first page of this story and remember "the past is a different country." They did things differently then but the Rotary Four Way Test is unchanged.

1. Is it the TRUTH
2. Is it FAIR to all concerned
3. Will it build GOODWILL and BETTER FRIENDSHIPS
4. Will it be BENEFICIAL to all concerned

List of Characters

Bartholomew Barratt QC	London based barrister
Samuel Bradshaw QC	Prosecution Barrister
George Brownlow	Local Police Sergeant
Mary Brownlow	Wife of the above
Major Calley	Bell Ringer and golfer
Doctor Carrington	The local Doctor
Jane Clayton	Stables Manager
DCI Raymond Crawford	Investigating Officer
Archibald Daltry	PHF Solicitor, Rotarian and a Bell Ringing Church Warden
DC Ted Egan	Dorset Constabulary Officer
Raynor Goddard	Lord Chief Justice
Emily Henderson	Elderly Church Warden
Oliver Henderson	Niece of above
Mrs Hinton	A farmer's wife
WPC Jackson	Dorset Constabulary Officer
Sam Loxton	Owner of the Lyydcastle Stores
Moira Mackenzie	Bell Ringer and District Nurse
Mrs Mannion	Home help to Rev O'Donnell
John O'Donnell	Vicar of St Anselm's
Miss Railton	Archibald Daltry's Secretary
Ronald Redpath	Pupil Barrister
Miss Standish	Matron of Woodside Lodge
Tom Wilkins	Bell Ringer and Church Warden

Chapter One

Sermons and Sherbet Lemons

Lyddcastle was a small village stretching towards the cliff tops. It had two roads. One ran roughly North to south linking Lyddcastle to Swanage in the South and Poole via a chain ferry to the North. The other ran down hill to the village of Studland and then across the spine of the isle of Purbeck to Corfe.

It was a lovely Spring morning. As the Vicar of St Anselm's fastened his dog collar in an upstairs bedroom, the paperboy sped past on his bike. It was a Friday. This being one of the days when Mrs Mannion did not come to the Vicarage and having finished dressing, the Vicar descended the stairs and set to making his own breakfast. As he buttered the two thick slices of toast, he could hear the bell ringers engaging in their weekly practice, which began at 7.30a.m. and lasted for an hour. It meant early rising for them, but was the one time when all the bell ringers were free of work, domestic or Rotary commitments. He did not believe the stories about bell ringing saving ships or as omens of good fortune, but they were a reassuring sound giving the feeling that God was in his heaven and all was right with the world.

In St Anselm's Church, the practice having concluded, the ringers dispersed leaving one of their number, who was also the church gardener, to lock the church and begin his work tending the graveyard. At about 9.45a.m. Miss Henderson, a church warden, came up the path carrying two large baskets of flowers.

"Good morning, Thomas," she said, pronouncing the word Thomas in a way that was both friendly but with an air of superiority. "Can't stop to talk this morning, I have to meet someone and I need to get these flowers done."

She let herself in through the main door of the church using a large old fashioned type key to unlock a rectangular wooden door set within a much larger one which filled the whole of the archway in the stonework. Old Tom, as he was known to everyone except Miss Henderson, returned to clipping grass round the stones that stood alongside the path from the gate to the main church door.

At about five past nine John O'Donnell, the vicar of St Anselm's, having finished his breakfast, left the Vicarage and walked to the village shop. He went to buy a bottle of wine, which was not for personal consumption, but for the Holy Communion Service he would hold on Sunday. It was his practice to make all the preparations for Sunday services on Friday, as with weddings and christenings one could never be sure of a clear day on a Saturday.

"Looks like the 9.05 is late," he said, by way of conversation to Sam Loxton behind the counter, observing a small queue of three or four people at the bus stop across the road. For some reason, the words of the hymn *"gave us eyes to see them and lips that we might tell"* ran through his head. It seemed like a celestial sign and turning his head back to the counter declared "and I will have a quarter of sherbet lemons if I may."

With the later purchase safely tucked in his raincoat pocket, he left the shop and headed for his church, St Anselm's. The church was named in honour of a Benedictine monk, one of whose followers had come here to live as a hermit and to be close to God. Getting to the church from the village shop meant retracing his steps, for although the church, like the village shop, was only a two minute walk from the Vicarage it was in the opposite direction. Arriving at the Gate, and not wanting to be engaged in a conversation with Old Tom, he hastily took himself up to the green Vestry door, unlocked it and let himself in closing it carefully behind him. The only hook in the Vestry was covered by his ecclesiastical garments so he went in to the main church and draped his raincoat over the choir stall. Returning to the Vestry he took some paper out of his desk. Taking and, uncapping his pen, he prepared to sit down and begin drafting his sermon for the Sunday service. Feeling inside his breast pocket, he was annoyed to find he had left his reading glasses back at the Vicarage. He could write perfectly well without them, however, and, if he needed to check an exact biblical quotation, he could refer to the bible on the lectern in the church which had large enough print for him to read unaided by spectacles. Thus, having reassured himself, he settled down to his sermon which was based on the conflicts that following the Ten Commandments can create for Christians and worked away happily for around half an hour. He was quite pleased with himself for having found instances, where biblical heroes did not always follow the commandments, and scribbled busily away. When he came to write about Judith's killing of Holofernes, he decided to use the actual biblical verses and got up and went in to the church to get the correct reference.

As he entered, he saw a figure clad in a grey jacket and matching bonnet who appeared to be looking into the font. He realised by the combination of small stature and smart grey outfit it could only be Miss Henderson and, desperate to avoid being seen by the lady, which would inevitably result in a lecture about parts of the church that ought to be repaired which he knew jolly well but had no way of financing, he attempted to remain unseen. Unfortunately, in the attempt he slipped on the thread bare carpet and struck his forehead on the side of the lectern. It was a fearful crack and quite disconcerted him. He was unsure whether he actually lost consciousness for a moment or two, but was soon aware that it hurt like hell. He staggered back to the vestry and began holding a handkerchief to his head. Almost dreading to look, he found the skin had not been broken and apart from some tenderness and an emerging lump of bruising, he did not seem to have suffered any permanent harm. He was also a little amazed that Miss Henderson had not heard but, guessing she was not wearing her hearing aids, gave thanks that he was going to be able to complete his sermon undisturbed, albeit with a rather sore head.

It was not to be though. Around ten o'clock he heard a most dreadful shriek from the main body of the church.

"Miss Henderson. Miss Henderson what's the matter are you alright?" The voice was that of Mrs. Hinton. She had arrived to polish the church silver and, as Old Tom let her in through the main church door, she saw Miss Henderson in a position which must have caused her to think she was trying to drown herself in the font. Old Tom had rushed in and hauling the slumped figure upright and finding her apparently lifeless, laid her gently on the ground at the side of the font.

"For heaven's sake someone get the Doctor.", shouted Mrs Hinton. Although, by this time, the Rev O'Donnell had come rushing down the aisle to where the font was, it was Old Tom who was quickest to react and hurried off for the nearest phone box.

Glancing down at the figure lying by the font, the Vicar spoke saying "if I am not mistaken, I am afraid it's too late. If I am not mistaken, she is dead. Our dear Sister will soon receive her heavenly reward."

Chapter Two

The Doctor's Diagnosis

There then followed an uncomfortable period waiting for the Doctor which Old Tom was spared, having been sent to get the Doctor while the Vicar and Mrs. Hinton were left with the inert body.

"She'll be like some of them lambs when they are born," said Mrs. Hinton. The farmer's wife seemed to be in a state of denial. "You think they is dead and then breathe in their mouth and swing em around and they is jumping all over the place."

The Vicar went and got his raincoat to cover Miss Henderson's body. He was realistic enough to know it would do no good, but it gave him something to do and it felt like a compassionate act. For good measure, he took a couple of cushions from a pew and placed them under Miss Henderson's head. While he had no intention of swinging Miss Henderson about like Miss Hinton's lambs, he grasped the body round the throat searching for a pulse. He found none. He had no idea how to perform artificial respiration but prepared to make an attempt. Pinching the nose was part of it and he tried to force the mouth open and made an attempt to blow. He soon gave up, whether because of his incompetence or the fact that she was well and truly dead, Miss Henderson remained inert.

Fortunately, Doctor Carrington was at home and not taking a surgery. Had there been less urgency he could well have walked from Holly Tree Cottage, the building that was both his home and surgery, and it took little more than a couple of minutes before his car drew up outside the church. Old Tom met him at the church gate and followed a respectful two paces behind as they strode up the path.

Once in the church, Dr Carrington exuded an air of calm authority. He knelt down beside the body and gently unfastened a cameo brooch which buttoned up the top of Miss Henderson's blouse. The hand whose fingers slid to the side of the throat to feel for a pulse were not those of a surgeon. They had done life-saving work in the Blitz though and, the rough skin and scars, bore witness to the fact that it had been moving burning rafters rather than wielding a scalpel that was the method by which he had saved lives. The Doctor shook his head and taking a torch out of his small black bag shone it in to Miss Henderson's eyes without getting any reaction from them.

"I'm sorry," he said "there's nothing I can do for the poor lady."

"But why Doctor?" asked Mrs Hinton.

"I'm sorry to say because she has died."

The Doctor gave the face of Miss Henderson a cursory glance and felt round behind the back of her head. "I have little doubt it was a heart attack. She was one of my patients and on medication. I must admit it is a surprise as she had never given any signs of heart disease but she was eighty five."

"Will there need to be a, what is it the Americans say? an autopsy?" The use of what he viewed as an Americanism seemed somehow disrespectful and John O'Donnell wished he had not voiced it.

"Not if I sign the death certificate to the effect that death was due to a myo cardial infarction. That's a heart attack in simple terms. I shall certainly be prepared to do so, unless any of you feel there should be a second opinion."

"I am sure that shouldn't be necessary, Doctor. Everyone in the village has the greatest trust in you and I hate to think of dear old Miss Henderson's body being exposed to prying eyes and cut about."

"I could not agree more Vicar," agreed the Doctor. I saw enough mangled corpses in the Blitz. Let this dear old soul's body go to its grave intact."

Old Tom and Mrs. Hinton nodded in agreement and the Doctor, having agreed to arrange for an ambulance to collect the body of the deceased, was about to leave when he gave John O'Donnell a curious look.

"That's a nasty shiner you have Vicar."

The Vicar put his hand on the aforementioned lump. "My goodness, I didn't think it had swollen that badly. I must have knocked it earlier this morning."

War time experience had instilled in the Doctor a desire to help the living more than the dead and he insisted the Vicar sit down on a pew while he inspected the lump both visually and tactilely, the latter causing a loud "ouch" from the Vicar. Doctor Carrington asked the Vicar how many fingers he could see and when he correctly announced three and received in reply to another question that it was Friday he smiled.

"You do not seem to have done yourself any serious damage. If you get a headache, take a couple of aspirins and if that doesn't have any effect you ought to have an x ray, but I don't think that will be necessary. If you haven't broken the skin, it's unlikely anything underneath is damaged."

Having again assured everyone that he would contact the hospital and use his contacts to see Miss Henderson was properly looked after, until the funeral directors were known and could take charge of her, Doctor Carrington waved a farewell and left.

Old Tom, the Vicar and Mrs. Hinton were all in accord that someone ought to stay with the body until it was collected and all three having expressed a willingness to do so, it was decided they would all stay. Old Tom had suggested "a brew", his solution to most of life's problems, and retired to the back of the church to make it, while his companions found themselves a couple of collapsible chairs to sit on.

The Vicar was feeling rather guilty about having seen Miss Henderson slumped over the font and ignoring her. Perhaps, he wondered to himself, if I had been a little more sociable I could have done something. It was not wanting to reveal that he had been in the main body of the church and seen Miss Henderson half an hour before the alarm was raised, that had made him rather reticent about explaining precisely how he had come to sustain the swelling on his forehead.

His quiet contemplation was interrupted by Old Tom returning with two mugs of tea, one blue and white patterned one he passed to Mrs. Hinton, the other, a Festival of Britain commemorative one, he gave to the Vicar. "There we are lady and gentleman the cup that cheers, even at such a sad time." With that, he retired to get his own drinking vessel, a battered tin mug that had kept him company in the trenches in one war and in an ARP Wardens' Hut in another.

They sat in a companionable silence. The Vicar felt in his pocket and considered offering them a sherbet lemon, but somehow eating sweets hardly seemed appropriate. Feeling in his pocket he felt a pair of glasses, but was unable to get them out.

Eventually, he realised that the reading glasses he had thought were back at the Vicarage had gone through a tear in the lining of his breast pocket and slipped down. Awkwardly, he retrieved them.

"Do you think a prayer would be in order?" he asked. Not being a Catholic, there could be no question of last rites, but just sitting as though you were waiting for a coal delivery seemed wrong and it did need something to make the time go more quickly.

"I would say that's a right good idea, Vicar," agreed old Tom. "I'm sure the old girl would like that and there were no one she would rather have reading it than you Vicar."

Mrs. Hinton seemed far away in a trance like state so John O'Donnell went back to his Vestry to fetch a bible, his mind burning with guilt that someone, so kind and fond of him, had been left when he might just have done something to save her. Returning, he put his glasses on and, while the others sat with suitably bowed heads, read a couple of Psalms beginning with the twenty third.

Chapter Three

The Bell Ringers Meeting

That Friday evening happened to be the one on which the monthly meeting of the Bell ringers took place in the Traveller's Return, a thatched hostelry not far from the church.

Like the Bankes Arms in nearby Studland, it owed its name to that family. The legend was that William Bankes, had been forced to flee abroad after being caught in a compromising situation in London's Green Park with a Guardsman in 1841. Exiled, he had roamed the continent sending back many valuable Treasures to his family home at Kingston Lacy. Rumour had it that, shortly before his death in 1855, he returned incognito and was able to spend a brief time in his homeland and viewed the treasures he had brought back to Kingston Lacy. The Traveller's Return had taken its name in his honour, although there was no evidence to suggest this was where he stayed or indeed if he had ever returned at all. This had not stopped the designer of the Inn sign depicting a moonlight scene, with a gentleman in Georgian costume being helped ashore by a piratical looking seaman.

The stated reason when the meetings had begun was to arrange duties for the coming month, but it had come to be a convivial social event and a chance to have a relaxed evening with fellow Campanologists. The bell ringers gathered around the table were five in number, four men and one woman, who was the District

Nurse, Moira Mackenzie. She served the whole of Purbeck, but had chosen this spot to live because of its centrality to the area she served and the beauty and seclusion of its position. She had been born in Scotland, but had come to know and love the area on holidays with her parents. She had always vowed that, if at all possible, she would return here to live. Hence, having achieved her nursing qualification and gained some experience in Edinburgh, she applied for and obtained the position of District Nurse for the area. Now in her early thirties, she seemed extremely happy and satisfied with life.

That said the like the rest of the ringers she was in a sombre mood as they dealt with what they would do in relation to Miss Henderson's funeral. Only the previous year the church had obtained a new set off mufflers just in time to mark the passing of King George. Not being a monarch, the bells would only be half muffled for Miss Henderson but the newest recruit, Sam Loxton's son, Danny would be sent up to the belfry to fix them. Unseen to any but themselves, a private tribute reserved for bell ringers and church wardens would be the attaching of black ribbon to the sallies, a custom begun by a previous Tower Captain.

Having agreed that whatever else happened they would have a full turn out for Miss Henderson's funeral whenever it was, it was perhaps not surprising that the conversation should centre on that lady. They were all in agreement that, had it not been for her tireless efforts organising fetes, not to mention a sizeable personal donation, the church bells would probably have remained silent after the War. It was genuine concern, rather than prurient curiosity, that saw the conversation turn to the events of the morning and their consequences.

"It's dam bad luck for the nephew," said Major Calley. "He does not come down here very often and when he does, he finds she's a goner. Still, I expect a lot of people round here will miss her, although she was a good age."

"That's true," interjected Nurse Mackenzie. She seemed to hesitate, and then thinking that Miss Henderson was not a patient and she was not broadcasting medical information, continued "but Miss Standish up at the Nursing Home will be a mite relieved, Miss Henderson was threatening to get the Inspectors in. Practically accused the Nursing Home of doing her sister in. It was ridiculous, of course, her sister had only gone in because of failing health and the longer she lived the more money the Nursing Home would make. Anyway, I told her, she was ninety- three and the death certificate showed there was nothing amiss.

"Who signed it?" asked old Tom.

"Why Doctor Carrington of course. He's the Doctor for all the residents at Woodside Lodge."

"Well taint worth much then," responded Tom.

Seeing a fellow medic, who was very well thought of by most of those patients she attended, being belittled roused Nurse Mackenzie's hackles.

"That is most uncalled for Mr. Wilkins. The Doctor is a very well-respected physician as you should know."

"No one is saying he bain't a good Doctor, but he is a man created by his experience same as me. When you have seen the bodies we have, him in the blitz, me in the trenches, you accept a dead man's a dead man and no altering it. Best get on and find some poor soul you can still help. Best ways by healing em, least ways by giving something to ease their pain, for good if necessary. Why he did no more than give Miss Henderson a passing glance once he knew er were dead. He showed more interest in that "shiner" of the Vicar.

"Do you mean to tell me that Mr. O'Donnell had a black eye?" The voice was that of Archibald Daltry, who, unlike the other four members of the group, who were clutching pints of Palmers ale, had in front of him a small sherry, which he alternatively sniffed and sipped. Archibald was a solicitor and the greatest living expert on Sir Reginald Palgrave, a local man who had been Clerk to the House of Commons for forty years. He was a generally acknowledged authority on the conduct of public meetings and the comment, "It would never have done for Sir Reginald" was one that Archibald was all too fond of using.

"Reckon he has now", said Tom, "then it were more of a big lump"

"So unseemly!" It was clear by the tone that the distaste shown by the solicitor was for a Vicar having been so careless as to sustain such an injury, rather than the taste of the sherry. "He always seems to be letting the side down in some way or other." It was unfortunate for John O'Donnell that he had replaced an extremely popular minister, who had retired after a long and valued ministry. Added to this, the solicitor's dislike of the new Vicar of St Anselm's was, in no small-measure, due to the fact that while the Church of England may be "a broad church," the Vicar and solicitor were situated at divergent locations within it.

"I suppose we should be grateful for the fact that he was not found cradling her in his arms. In my opinion, he was far too friendly with some of his lady parishioners."

"Come on old chap," broke in the Major "it is no more than Christian charity to befriend widows and elderly spinsters. Like several of the fair sex, Miss Henderson liked nothing better than having someone round for a meal, especially since her sister died. I can't see there was anything sexual in it, not at her age."

"Well said Major," responded Nurse Mackenzie. "Miss Henderson really enjoyed the Vicar's company. Even Casanova did not chase after eighty -five year olds, let alone our Vicar, who gets flustered if he sees a glimpse of cleavage."

"Even so, there should be a certain distance between a Shepherd and his flock," broke in Archibald. "I never suggested there was anything of a sexual nature, but I wouldn't put a financial interest past him. He was always complaining about the miserly nature of the church, both in regards to his own wages and funding church repairs. The real tragedy is that Miss Henderson may not see her finances distributed as she would have wished."

"What makes you say that?" queried the Major, "she always seemed such a well organised person. I can't believe she did not have a will."

"Oh, she had a will alright," confirmed Mr. Daltry, who was her solicitor, "but she had made an appointment to see me next Tuesday to change it. Don't ask me how or why she was going to change it because I don't know, and don't ask me what is in the current one either because it's confidential." Whether because of a fear he would be pressed on the matter or merely because of the time, he finished his sherry and bade farewell to his fellow bell ringers.

The Major offered to get another round in, but there was a general sense around the table that the usual enjoyment of their monthly meeting was not there tonight and people indicated they would soon be making tracks themselves. Nurse Mackenzie was clearly concerned though. "All this suspicion. I'm sure it's rubbish, but is there no way we can get it confirmed that poor old Miss Henderson died of a heart attack?"

Sergeant George Brownlow was the only bell ringer who had remained silent during the discussion of Miss Henderson's demise. In a big city constabulary, he would probably have been a disaster waiting to happen and, his tendency to believe the best of everybody, a liability. In a quiet rural back water, where the biggest crime was usually riding a bike with no lights, and the greatest mystery how Farmer Hinton's cows got out on the road, he was ideal. His quiet easy-going nature could not have been more suited to, what he liked to call, "his patch".

He always thought the fact that we had two ears, two eyes and one mouth was a hint as to how we should behave but what he had heard with his ears in this conversation justified saying something. "I hear what you are saying Moira I think it would be in everyone's best interest if we could get it confirmed as a heart attack. What I would hate to happen though is anyone thinking we are questioning Dr Carrington's judgement. I can't think he would make a mistake. Can I ask you all not to say anything about the matter? I have an old colleague who might just be able to help, without any fuss or post mortem nonsense. Leave it with me." Having said his piece, the Sergeant. took his leave and was soon followed by the others, all of whom seemed in a more relaxed frame of mind, knowing whatever happened it was in the hands of a down to earth local man they all trusted.

Chapter Four

A series of phone calls

On reaching home, having greeted his wife and asked her to hold back their supper for ten minutes, he made a phone call to a Detective Inspector Crawford. They had worked together when Roger Crawford was a young PC, and although he had stayed in the local area, Roger's sharp mind and ambitious attitude had seen him rise through the ranks.

The conversation went like this

RC. Wareham 347

GB. Detective Inspector Crawford?

RC Speaking

GB. Sergeant Brownlow speaking, I wonder if you might be able to help?

RC. Well, my word, George old friend. How are you?

GB. Fine

RC. The wife?

GB. Mary's fine too

RC. Glad to hear it. Now what can I do for you? I doubt I would be where I am today had it not been for the good grounding you gave me. I'll certainly help if I can.

GB. Well in one way it's a bit awkward and it's probably something or nothing.

You see, we had an old lady die suddenly this morning. It was probably a natural death, as she was 85, but people are gossiping and these things can fester and create bad feelings and suspicions unless there is something concrete to show they are wrong.

RC. What did the Doctor say?

GB. He said it was a heart attack and he was there pretty quickly.

RC. What's the problem then?

GB. Well, one or two people who were there or know his history seem to think he is a bit too quick in his judgements. Nine times out of ten I expect he is right, but, it sounded as though he was a bit too quick to assume a probability as a certainty as it were.

RC. So how can I help?

GB. I just wondered if there is anyway, unofficial like, that you could get a second opinion.

RC. Could be awkward. Where is the body at the moment?

GB. Dr Carrington arranged for her to be taken to the hospital until the Funeral Directors could collect her so I expect she is still there.

RC. You might just be in luck then. The pathologist is due there to do a post mortem on a hit and run victim. If I stand him a full English in the canteen I expect I can persuade him to have a look.

GB. Thanks. It would be a weight of my mind if you did. It was something aSolicitor said when we had a bell-ringers meeting just now. Apparently, Miss Henderson had booked an appointment to see him to change her Will. Probably made me put two and two together and make five.

RC. Yes, probably coincidence, but best make sure.

GB . Many thanks

The next morning, Chief Inspector Crawford was as good as his word. Having consumed a hearty breakfast, the Pathologist, having warned he could not do any carving without an official form, looked at the body with his expert eye. This resulted in a return conversation between the Chief Inspector and Sergeant. Brownlow just after lunchtime.

RC. Is that you GB?

GB. Yes sir. Hello, any news?

RC. Indeed, there is, but I am going to ask you to keep what I tell you in confidence for the time being.

GB. If you say so, but how is that going to help us stop the rumours spreading and confirming it was a heart attack that did for poor old Miss Henderson?

RC. That's just it. It wasn't. For once your arithmetic of putting two and two together and making five was right. It appears she was killed.

GB. You mean someone murdered her?

RC   At present, it's a matter for the coroner and I would prefer to term it a suspicious death, although, given my Pathologist friend is pretty certain she was suffocated, it's difficult to see how it could have been an accident. He examined her eyes and the blood shot nature of them made him suspicious.

He did a test on the level of carbon dioxide in the blood and he reckoned that proved it conclusively. Anyway, it was sufficient that when I told the Chief Constable. He ordered a coroner's inquest and has put me on the case. Are you working tomorrow?

GB   No, it's Sunday and a rest day for me, but I will happily meet you.

RC. Excellent, how about twelve o'clock in the Travellers Arms?

GB. Fine, you are welcome to come round for lunch if you fancy it.

RC. I would, but I want to get moving on as many fronts as I can, so thanks but thanks. There is one thing you could do for me though. Can you sort out with your bell ringing solicitor friend an appointment for me to see him onMonday morning.

GB. I'll get on to it right away, what should I say it's for?

RC. Just say I've been asked to look in to Miss Henderson's demise ready for the Coroner.

GB. Right you are. Look forward to seeing you tomorrow. Bye for now.

Chapter Five

Sunday morning

One of the reasons for Roger Crawford's rapid promotion was his willingness to put in the extra mile in his own time and it was this habit which saw him making a trip the next morning, earlier than he need have done so, to see Sergeant Brownlow, and, despite being off duty, to pay a visit to the morning service at St Anselm's church to, as he explained to his wife, "kill two birds with one stone and get a feel of the place where it happened, as well as see his old friend George."

He followed an elderly couple down the church path passing grave stones that, despite their age, were so upright that he almost expected them to salute. Between them daffodils, sprouted giving promise of new life and bringing an air of continuity to the scene. As he was walking down the path the lone tolling of the Sanctus bell had begun so the church was already quite full. Entering the church, he found a seat just over half way back where he had a better view of the font than the pulpit, and settled back to make a mental note of anything he thought might have a bearing on the case. The main body of the church and its side aisles had an open aspect and were fronted to the left by an eagle lectern and to the right by a pulpit reached by climbing a short circular staircase, covered in a threadbare carpet.

The service itself consisted of three hymns, a couple of readings and a sermon. It was the latter which most caught the ear of the Chief Inspector. The planned, but never completed homily on the Ten Commandments, had been abandoned and it was the passing of Miss Henderson that formed the focus of much of what the Vicar said. Chief Inspector Crawford learnt that the lady had been St Anselm's Senior Church Warden and that her floral arrangements, made with flowers from her own garden, would be much missed. He found the sermon strangely reassuring with its message of resurrection and reunion. "Rest assured," said the Reverend O'Donnell, "we will meet our dear sister Emily.

Now she rests in peace and will, in due course, rise in glory along with all the faithful and not so faithful." He went on to talk about how recent months had seen the passing of those of different stations, including the Queen's grandmother in this country and the Russian leader, Joseph Stalin in another. "The Lord has gathered them all in, although perhaps it is well that the Lord's House has many mansions, for, one wonders, how Mr. Stalin would respond to being told to wipe his muddy boots before coming in, by Miss Henderson. But such things are not of importance, for this world, as St Augustine tells us, is but a poor reflection of the World to come."

It was only as the organist was striking up the first chords of "Glorious things of thee are spoken," that Roger Crawford reflected on another passage in the sermon. This had been specifically directed at Miss Henderson's passing. The Vicar had spoken of "a good life, earning a right to a peaceful passing in a place she adored among friends she loved." It left one thinking that, from the Vicar's point of view, whoever killed her had almost been doing her a good turn.

Leaving quickly at the end of the service, so as to avoid the ritual handshakes and farewell to the Vicar, he took a walk around the tower end of the church. He satisfied himself that apart from the main entrance the only other way in to the church was a green door on the same side. The stained-glass windows which looked so attractive inside had a darker aspect seen from outside but, more importantly from his detective's perspective, they had no means of being opened. He strolled down to the far end of the graveyard to look out over the green hills to the white chalk headland and the blue sea beyond. Anyone coming up this way would be visible but it seemed an unlikely way of access, given there were no houses but just a couple of fields occupied by cattle, who munched lazily and in a disinterested fashion. Realising the time for his meeting with Geoff Brownlow was rapidly approaching, he turned and walked back alongside the hedge that separated the church grounds from the neighbouring farm.

Arriving in the Bankes Arms, Roger Crawford found the Sergeant at the bar. Accepting the offer of a drink it being lunch time, he asked for a tonic water with a dash of lime. The main bar was fairly busy and Geoff suggested they retired to a small rather windowless area. On Tuesday and Thursday nights it was the preserve of the pub darts team, but otherwise it offered the properties of what might well have been termed a snug.

They chatted amiably for some twenty minutes about family, friends and former work mates before, having got in a further tonic water for himself and the half pint requested by his friend, Roger got out his note book.

"I must admit George, half the reason for seeing you is to hope you might be able to fill me in on things that might help the investigation."

"That's not a problem," responded George, "Anything in particular?"

"Well, basically, when did you find out about Miss Henderson's death and do you know who found her?"

George explained how it was only when he had met with his fellow bell ringers that he had been told by Tom, who he said worked in the church yard. Beyond that, he warned, what he had learnt was basically second-hand but had all come from the same source which he had no reason to disbelieve. "According to old Tom, Miss Henderson had arrived at the church about a quarter to nine. She was carrying a basket of cut flowers and let herself in. She's the Head Church Warden so has her own key to the main church entrance. He reckoned it was the best part of an hour later that Mrs. Hinton arrived and it was she who raised the alarm. By the time Tom had got in the church hearing her cries, the Vicar was there as well. He seemed to think Miss Henderson was dead, but sent Tom to get the Doctor. The Doctor came fairly quickly, living just round the corner like, and it was he who pronounced Miss Henderson having died as the result of a heart attack. Then the three of them; that's Tom, the Vicar and Mrs. Hinton stayed with the body until the ambulance came. Like I say though, it's only what Tom said. You will need to talk to the other two to verify it.

"I will," reassured the Inspector, "but it's a great help because it points me in the right direction. When did you first get suspicious that it might not be a heart attack?"

"Well, old Tom went on about the Doctor being a bit careless and not worrying exactly about why a person died, but I still didn't think anything of it. It was when Archie Daltry mentioned about Miss Henderson having booked an appointment to see him about a new will, but you could still have knocked me down with a feather when you told me she had been murdered. Oh, by the way, I hope it's alright, but you asked me to book an appointment with my bell ringing solicitor friend for you. he is free at 9.30a.m. tomorrow morning so I asked him to keep it free to see you. I hope that's convenient."

"Indeed, it is. By the way, one last thing, do you happen to know if Miss Henderson had any relatives?"

"She had a nephew. I think he's a student up at Oxford. If you need to get in touch with him Major Calley's your best bet. He's one of our bell ringers. He was saying he was coming down here this weekend. They play golf together. I think the Major was friends with his father, when they were in India together."

Smiling, the Inspector thanked George for this information, commenting on how it would save him a few phone calls, before departing and leaving his friend to return to his wife and Sunday roast.

Chapter Six

Miss Henderson's Will

A nine thirty appointment meant an early start for Roger Crawford as he needed to call at the station to collect DC Ted Egan, who had been assigned to help him for the week, before he made the journey to Swanage to see the solicitor in his office.

The lawyer had agreed to an early appointment, due to concern and curiosity. The two emotions were present in equal measure, as he tried to take control of the meeting by escorting the two officers in to his office and offering them tea or coffee. DI Crawford declined politely, commenting on having had a couple of cups at breakfast, and the DC tactfully followed suit. The solicitor had intended to ask the purpose of the officers' visit but, before he could do so, it was volunteered by Roger Crawford.

"We are much obliged to you for seeing us so promptly. The Chief Constable has asked me to make sure we have gathered all the facts together for the Coroner. It's a routine visit. We have not had the results of the post mortem yet." It was a wonderful example of telling nothing but the truth but not the whole truth, as it left out the fact that the Police Pathologist was almost certain Miss Henderson's death had been the result of suffocation.

Daltry pulled nervously at the end of his shirt sleeves and waited.

"It was one of your bell ringing colleagues that mentioned Miss Henderson had made an appointment to see you about making a will."

There was an almost imperceptible relaxation of the solicitor's shoulders as he realised the visitation from this high ranking police officer apparently saw him as an informant rather than a suspect. "That's certainly true. She rang my Secretary, who had booked her in to see me tomorrow."

"Did she have a will already?" asked Crawford.

"Yes, she made it a couple of years ago. Evidently she wanted to make some changes to it."

"Did you know what these changes related to?" pressed the Inspector.

"I am afraid not, she just told Miss Railton, my secretary, she was thinking of making some changes."

"Changes to her existing will?", Crawford continued in his search for information.

"Now there I can help you. My firm holds a copy of the will and I got it out and had Miss Railton, make a copy so we would each have one when Miss Henderson came, in to discuss it. We won't be needing the copy now so you are welcome to take it away, although I would ask you to keep it confidential until the main beneficiaries have been informed. I should inform you that my firm are the executors and we intend to read the will to beneficiaries by the end of the week. Apart from some small bequests of jewellery and some money set aside for a bench in the Churchyard, the estate is to be divided equally between her nephew, Mr. Oliver Henderson, the Reverend John O'Donnell and the Woodside Lodge Nursing Home."

"Can I ask how much, roughly speaking, a third of the estate will amount to?" enquired the DCI.

"There are considerable numbers of investments to be realized so it is is difficult to be accurate. Of course, given that Miss Henderson inherited the entire estate of her sister, who sadly died earlier this year, it will be a sizeable amount."

The Chief Inspector had another question. "Do you happen to know who the owners of the Woodside Lodge Nursing Home are?"

The solicitor shook his head sadly, "I am afraid not. It was set up by the present matron's father. He was a Doctor. I imagine she will certainly be involved in some shape or form. I must say it will be an absolute godsend for them. So much of what they charge for you they can now get for free on the National Health, so times are tough for them."

Looking at his colleague, Roger said, "Unless you have any questions DC Egan, I think that will be all. Thank you it's been of great assistance."

Pleased the meeting was over and gaining in confidence, Archibald Daltry reached for the phone and asked his secretary to let the officers have a copy of the will she had made. "One more thing gentlemen. I find myself in a difficult position and feel I should mention it before somebody else does. You see as executors of the will, who Miss Henderson leaves her money to is very much her own business and no concern of mine. However, as a church Warden of St Anselm's it is."

Crawford interposed, hoping it would make the solicitor confident of speaking more freely. "Like yourself Sir, we in the force have a code of ethics and nothing that is not pertinent to our inquiries will be shared with anyone else by myself or my colleague."

"Thank you for that Gentlemen. You see I did not feel it was entirely appropriate that Miss Henderson should leave such a large sum of money to an employee of the church."

"Had you shared this view with Miss Henderson?" asked the Chief Inspector.

"Not directly, no. I should also add that I only felt able to speak of it as Miss Henderson made no secret of it herself. She used to joke with the Vicar that when she got her heavenly reward, he would not have to worry about affording sherbet lemons any more. Given her openness, I felt it was not a breach of confidentiality to bring it to the attention of the Deacon. You see, to me it would be entirely proper to leave a legacy of this size to the church itself, to leave it to the Vicar himself though, does not seem quite right to me. It could lead to Miss Henderson's relationship with him being seen in quite the wrong light."

"Do you think that might be why she wanted to change the Will?"

"I honestly do not know. Once she set her mind on something she was very determined, but why she wanted to see me about a change I just can't think," said the lawyer, who emphasized his point with a shake of the head.

Armed with a copy of the Will, which Roger Crawford slipped in to his breast pocket, the two officers took their leave and were soon driving back towards Lyddcastle. In the car, Crawford explained to Ted Egan that he had arranged to meet the Rev John O'Donnell at the Vicarage. He went on to say that he wanted Ted to knock on the doors of the houses between the Vicarage and the Church to see if anyone had seen anything on the Friday morning.

"Anything in particular you are looking for?" queried the DC.

"No keep it fairly vague. I am going to tell the Vicar we suspect foul play, but don't want to start a general rumour mill going. You could ask if they are worried about prowlers and suggest that we can always get an officer to come and look at their security. When you get to the church there are four or five houses between there and Cliff Tops, that's the house where Miss Henderson lives. Whichever of us gets there first can pop to the next-door neighbour. She's got the key for the house evidently."

Chapter Seven

A visit to the Vicarage

Arriving at the vicarage, Raymond Crawford walked up the gravel path. Reaching the door, which was adorned with a door knocker with a female head with long tresses, he rapped on it and the door opened. Standing before him was not the Vicar, but his part time home help, Mrs Mannion, evidently in the middle of her cleaning duties. Mrs Mannion was obviously not aware of plain clothes detectives being policemen but she bustled down a corridor and opened a door at the end calling across to a figure standing by the window. "That Mr Crawford you was on about is 'ere. Shall I do some tea or coffee?"

The DCI refused to divert Mrs Mannion from her duties, kind as he observed though the offer was. "The Reverend O'Donnell?" he asked.

The figure at the window nodded and indicated for his visitor to take a seat. The only place to do, so apart from the captain's type swivel chair situated behind a desk, was the far end of a sofa, the rest of which was covered with books and papers. The room, which evidently served as the Vicar's Office, had a lived in feel which bordered on the chaotic. Crawford's observant eye thought it strange therefore, when everything else in the room was in such a state of disorder, that a glass case containing candle snuffers had every item carefully spaced and aligned in a way which would have satisfied Hercule Poirot.

"What a lovely collection of candle snuffers," observed the detective.

"I am afraid it's my little weakness. Although most have been bought for me. I did a sermon about them once and now people seem to buy them for me. It can be a bit of an embarrassment. Jane Clayton buys me one every birthday and Christmas and I happen to know they are quite expensive ones."

"It must be nice to be appreciated"

"Yes, but it can give people the wrong idea. I suppose it is an occupational hazard to find some of your lady parishioners want to mother you which is bad enough, but others see you as an eligible bachelor which makes it difficult to draw the line between showing love as a Christian virtue without it seeming to be born of baser motives.

The Vicar was clearly uncomfortable so, adopting his usual approach of trying to put people at ease before engaging in pertinent questioning, the Inspector commented, "The garden looks lovely."

"Yes it does," agreed the Vicar, who had continued gazing out of the window. "It's the right time of year, nature's work rather than mine."

"Not St Anselm's though, from what I saw of it on Sunday that is well cared for by human hands." Crawford continued sensing a certain unease in the figure still staring out of the window.

The figure turned and sat down on the chair by his desk with head bowed almost in an attitude of prayer. "I do wish you would ask what you have come for. I'm not a twelve year old that's never had to deal with death before."

In was a sudden outburst and, equally swiftly, the Vicar suddenly changed his posture and began to look at the visitor instead of the floor. "I'm sorry that was uncalled for. It's kind of you to speak well of the church some people do so much to care for it and so few show appreciation, but Emily, I mean Miss Henderson's death has hit me hard."

"That's understandable. Did she mean a lot to you?" questioned Crawford.

"Not personally, although she did so much for the church heaven knows how we will replace her. It's the fact that we used to joke so often about death. I'd talk about how many sherbet lemons there would be in heaven and Miss Henderson would go on about earning her heavenly reward. We Christians ought to be able to do that, but now she's dead it seems rather improper."

Deciding to grasp the nettle, Crawford broke in on the Vicar's contemplations. "I think I should tell you that we do not think her death was the result of natural causes. We have not got the full post mortem results yet, but it seems extremely likely her death, at the very least, could be termed suspicious."

"But who on earth would want to poison her? I know some people found her tiresome in fact," O'Donnell broke off, "but why murder a poor old lady?"

"She was not that poor so we do have to consider someone might have had a financial motive."

At this point the conversation was interrupted by Mrs. Mannion who, having disregarded the two men's assurance they did not want anything to drink, was pushing a trolley containing a pot of tea, two cups and saucers and numerous biscuits.

"'Ere we are gents. The cup that cheers. The Reverence needs something to cheer him up, been proper peaky these last couple of days. Moping about won't ever do you no good, that's what I says."

With a heaving of his shoulders, the Vicar spoke. "Mrs. Mannion, you may not have wings but you are indeed an angel." Being grateful had come hard and was a bit wasted as, by this time, the recipient of the praise was making their way out of the door and back down the corridor.

"Will you join me Inspector?" asked the Vicar.

"Given the good lady's efforts to refuse would be churlish", responded Crawford.

Having ascertained the Inspector's requirement regarding milk and sugar the Vicar began to pour, carefully keeping the teapot lid secured with one hand. It gave the ever observant police officer the chance to study John O'Donnell's hands. They had clearly never been used for manual labour but looked otherwise firm and strong.

"Who was it found Miss Henderson?" asked Crawford, helping himself to a shortcake biscuit.

"It was Mrs. Hinton. I heard her cries of distress, and by the time I came out of the Vestry, Tom, one of the bell ringers who works in the churchyard, had also come in. He went to fetch the Doctor, but I had the feeling it was too late for them to be of any help."

In reply to further questions the Vicar estimated the time to be around ten o'clock and that he had arrived at the church himself about nine or just after. He then volunteered some further information. "I do feel awful about this death in my church. You see in a way I feel responsible. About half an hour before Mrs. Hinton alerted me, I had gone in to the church to look at the Bible on the lectern because I did not have my glasses. I had seen Miss Henderson bent over the font. If I had tried to speak to her, I would have realised something was wrong. I might have been able to help or fetch someone who could. She might still have been alive, but I really did not want to waste time. I just wanted to finish writing my sermon and get back to the Vicarage to do my own thing. It was selfish behaviour and now I shall have my dear Emily's death on my conscience."

The Inspector tried to reassure the Vicar that, although one could not be sure until the cause of death was confirmed, it was likely that when he saw her, Miss Henderson was already dead, before raising a query about access to the church. "Am I right in thinking there are only two entrances to the church? enquired Crawford, seeking confirmation for his observations after the Sunday service.

The Vicar confirmed this fact and then responded to a question about key holders. "The main entrance has three. Rather heavy cumbersome things. Of the three, one is allocated to the bell ringers, which Tom holds. Miss Henderson had one, as the Senior Church Warden, and I have the third. As to the Vestry, that has a Yale lock. It came with two keys and I have them both on the same ring. I should really either let someone else have it or at least put it somewhere else in case they get lost, but I've never got round to it."

"Well, I expect you are a busy man Vicar and it will mean one less person for us to worry about questioning if you have both the keys. Thank you for your time. I won't take up any more of it. I just wonder, do you know anything about Miss Henderson's nephew?"

The Inspector had got up to go and the Vicar also stood up before replying. "Apart from the fact that she had one, not much. I believe he is a student at Oxford, but your best bet would be to talk to Major Calley, he's one of our bell ringers. I believe he was friends with his father."

Thanking the Vicar he informed him, "Evidently so, as you are the second person to suggest that. Any way I am much obliged."

Realising the interview was at an end the Vicar politely showed the Inspector out before turning back and closing the door.

On his way down the path the Inspector made a couple of notes. He jotted down the timings the Vicar had given him before the names of the key holders and ended by writing the word POISON in capitals and putting a question mark after it. A crunching on the gravel path alerted him that Mrs. Mannion was walking down the drive. As much by way of politeness as from any expectation that it would yield any pertinent information, Crawford asked "Do you live locally Mrs. Mannion?"

"Very", came the response. "Just down the road past the church and round the bend. I don't even need to cross the road so there is no need to worry about me."

Realising that this would have meant she lived in one of the houses which Ted Egan had been detailed to carry out enquiries, the diligent Inspector seized the chance to fill in the gap. "So, you would have a good view of the churchyard. Did you see anything unusual on Friday morning?"

"Not that I can think off", she said seeming to ponder, "except, now you ask, there was Miss Henderson."

"So did she not usually come to the church on a Friday morning?", asked the Inspector, wondering if he may have stumbled on something.

"Oh no, she always came on a Friday. You see she likes to have the flowers looking fresh for any weddings on the Saturday and the services on Sunday. It was the time though. Usually, she comes along at ten o'clock on the dot, but she was much earlier. I couldn't say exactly, but it was before the nine o'clock news. I was doing the washing up and I always do that before the nine o'clock news."

"Can you think of any reason why?"

"You 'ave got me there, Constable. Perhaps she had an assignation with the Vicar. She was always very pally with him. Mind you, I can't imagine his Holiness being involved with any of 'that sort of thing.' More's the pity, he is a handsome man for his age and such lovely manners. There's more than one lady parishioner would happily take him up his own aisle or have a bit of 'that sort of thing' in his own vestry, if that were all that was on offer."

Crawford smiled inwardly at what was obviously the lady's euphemism for any sexual liaison but, suspecting he was not going to get any more worthwhile information, decided to bid the lady farewell and get in his car.

He drove the few hundred yards that took him down the road and parked up at Cliff Top House, the home of the late Miss Henderson, just in time to meet Ted Egan coming up the steep driveway to meet him. "It's alright Sir, I have got the key, mind you, not much else. One old chap reckoned he saw some tramp with a beard when he was out walking the dog, but his wife seems to think he might be making it up to get attention. She reckoned if she thought he could get someone to talk to him and buy him a pint he'd see whatever you wanted."

"Never mind, you have got the keys for Cliff Top House so let's see what we can find."

Cliff Top House justified its name for only a long lawn broken up by flowerbeds separated it from the very edge of the chalk cliff face. The downstairs consisted of a corridor running down its centre with rooms coming off on either side. The two police officers looked at each in turn but spent some time in one windowless room that seemed like a library, as one wall was completely covered by books on shelves. There were a number of religious works and a large collection of books and periodicals on gardening but most seemed to be military history books which had probably been here when Miss Henderson's father had been alive.

They had a little more success upstairs. The first room which Ted Egan described as "bloody creepy," had evidently been the bedroom of Miss Emily Henderson's sister, as the dressing table was covered with framed pictures of the lady around a fresh vase of flowers. Opening a drawer, Crawford found a bundle of letters. Undoing them he found they were letters of condolence. The bed itself looked ready for use but sensing there was nothing to be found, they closed the door and crossed to Emily Henderson's bedroom. A neat and tidy room, it gave Inspector Crawford the first item to put in what he termed his murder bag. On the bedside table were three bottles of tablets. One was a commercial bottle of paracetamol, while the other two were labelled as containing chemicals which had evidently been prescribed, but for what reason would require further investigation. All three bottles were about half full.

The final room was perhaps the nicest room in the house. Ted Egan went straight to the window exclaiming. "Now this is a room you could live in. Reminds me of upstairs in the Russell Coates Museum, only more spacious." While Egan was enjoying the view, the Inspector found something that he found more pertinent to the case in hand. On a leather topped table lay an open cash box containing two florins and a six-penny piece. Beside it was a cash book, which he picked up and inspected. Neatly entered in blue and red ink were items of income and expenditure with a balance at the end of each entry. It seemed more than coincidence that the balance after the last entry was 17 pounds four shillings and sixpence. Had someone removed the notes and left the small change?

The search complete and the key returned to the next-door neighbour, Crawford drove with Egan back to the station at Wareham. On the way, he explained he wanted to stay at the station on the morning of the next day to get the pathologist's report but he had some people he wanted Ted to contact and interview.

Parking up in the station car park, he turned to a clean sheet in his black flip top Police note book. "These are three people I want you to talk to tomorrow morning. When you have managed to see all three or at twelve o'clock if you are still working on it ring me at the station. I am afraid I have not got an address for the nephew, but you will find Mrs. Hinton at the Hinton's Farm and you should be able to track down Miss Standish at the Woodside Lodge Nursing Home where she is the matron."

Chapter Eight

Three Interviews

Having rung Major Calley the previous evening, by Tuesday morning Ted Egan was able to catch an early bus to Swanage where, the Major had informed him, he would find Oliver Henderson, Miss Henderson's nephew staying at a small hotel just off the sea front. An enquiry at reception saw him pointed to the Residents Lounge, where he found Mr Henderson reading a paper and enjoying a cup of coffee.

He explained the reason for his visit and was immediately invited to sit down. Putting down his newspaper, Oliver summoned a waiter who was asked to "be a good fellow and fetch another coffee for my guest."

Henderson gave the appearance of somebody who would have looked very fashionable, if he had been living in the nineteen thirties. He wore a brightly coloured cardigan over an open necked shirt and a pair of what were affectionately known as Oxford Bags. "Now old bean how can I be of help?" beamed the student.

"Well sir, I was just wondering if you could give me an account of your movements last Friday morning?"

"I thought dear old Aunt Em had died of natural causes but talking to Major Calley started me wondering and a policeman coming to see me makes me think that might not be the case."

"We are keeping an open mind at present Sir. Just have to get all the facts together for the Coroner."

"If it was not natural causes, it's dashed awkward as I don't think I've got an alibi, old sport. Let me tell you what happened. Thursday night we had an OUDS rehearsal."

"Sorry sir, what's OUDS?"

"The Oxford University Dramatic Society. We were rehearsing Oedipus Rex which is pretty bloody and would not have been my choice. I'm more of a "Charlie's Aunt" myself, but a chap needs to blow off a bit, so we went for a few snifters. The chap I am in college with was still fast asleep and, away with the fairies next morning, when I got up to come down here to see Aunt Em. I was a bit later starting as I meant to get away at six, but I woke up late and needed a coffee to wake myself up and set out about half past seven. Got the old jalopy out and started off. I had a good run but somewhere between Newbury and Ringwood, I felt a bit peckish: You see Thursday night we drank a lot but didn't eat much. So I think's to myself I could do with a good old English fry up, so I stopped at a cafe in a lay by and had bacon and eggs and a coffee. I'd better add I had a couple of aspirins for the old head. Anyway, whether it was the tablets or the breakfast I felt much better and completed my journey "tout suite" as the froggies say. I get to Cliff Top House about eleven but there was no sign of Aunt Em so I went and knocked at the house next door. Now, she's a queer cove if ever there was one. Well, I asked her if she knows where Miss Henderson next door is and she says you'll probably find her at the church. I asked her why she thought that and she said she always goes down to St Anselm's on Friday mornings and she particularly noticed she had left earlier than usual. So, I expected to find her, but blowed if I thought she would be being carried out stone cold dead.

Ted could hardly have asked for more and thanked Oliver for being so frank but thought there was one more thing that DI Crawford would want to know and so he asked "What made you decide to come down this weekend?"

"Well there, old bean, I have to admit to being "mea culpa". You see, her sister died just after Christmas and she had written to me to say she had to decide what to do with the money she had inherited from her. You see, being older and expecting to die first, her sister had left everything to Aunt Emily. What with the house being lived in by them both any other way might have caused problems. Well, reading between the lines, I got the feeling that there might be a bit of cash coming the way of yours truly, but if I couldn't be bothered to show an interest in Aunt Emily and what she was going to do with money then it might well end up with salmon for tea at the local cats' home but diddly squat pour moi. Now it looks like a bit of a wasted trip. Still, I shall fit in a couple of rounds of golf while I'm down here."

Ted thanked him and said he'd be on his way as he wanted to catch the next bus which went to Lyddcastle.

"No need for that," burst out Oliver, "I'm playing up at Purbeck this afternoon with the Major. Why don't I drop you of at Lyddcastle? It's not far out of my way and I will still have time for a bit of nosh at the club before our tee off time."

Ted was only too glad to accept and Oliver went off to his room to change and urged Ted to enjoy another coffee on him, while he did so. Ted was only too glad to follow this course and mused on whether he should visit the Nursing Home or the farm to see Mrs Hinton first. He had come to no decision on this when Oliver Henderson reappeared resplendent in plus fours and a Fair Isle sweater of a rather loud design. The pair left the hotel by the front door and made their way to Oliver's car.

The journey up to Lyddcastle was mainly occupied with Oliver asking whether Ted played golf. On receiving the reply that he didn't, but would like to try it, launched Oliver into a monologue about the joys of the game in general and the Isle of Purbeck course in particular. Just as they approached Lydcastle, an approaching tractor forced Oliver to break off his exposition on the problems of keeping the ball on the fairway in dry weather, to keeping his car on the road. Having done so successfully and his mind now back on his driving he asked "Whereabouts would you like me to drop you?" and received the reply that his passenger would like to speak to a lady at the Springfield Nursing Home. This was duly done, with a wave of the hand and a "toodle Pip, old bean" the driver reversed and departed with a spray of gravel.

Ted walked up the path to the grand but old fashioned door and rang a bell at its side. This did not seem to produce any response, so he looked more closely and saw a notice in the middle of the door which said PLEASE COME IN DURING DAYLIGHT HOURS. Turning the large circular knocker he found the door opened and he made his way inside. Immediately to his left was a door which had a plaque indicating it was the Matron's Office. As this was the lady he had come to see, he knocked on it. When there was no reply, he saw an open door across the corridor and went in. It was evidently some sort of staff rest room with a kettle and cups alongside a sink in one corner, with easy chairs and magazines scattered around. There was only one lady present and she was lolling in a chair, reading a magazine and smoking a cigarette.

"I wonder if you could help me at all, I'm looking for Miss Standish, the Matron. You would not happen to know if she is about would you?" Ted asked her.

"Afraid you have picked the wrong day. Tuesday is her day off. Can I help at all?"

"Probably not. You see I need to talk to her about the lady who died in the church last week. It's a matter of form really, but we have to account for certain people's whereabouts."

Stubbing out the remains of the cigarette and getting to her feet she declared, "Well this might help." Crossing the room, she tapped on a notice board. Moving to stand beside her, Ted saw she was pointing to a staff rota. It contains days divided into mornings 8 to 2 afternoons 2 until 8 and nights 8 to 8. Each rectangle contained the initials of the duty nurse, but alongside both the previous Friday morning and the preceding night was written the word Matron. Evidently, Miss Standish took her fair share of responsibility as befitted the leader, but by using her rank, rather than initials, was not shy of making the fact and her rank known to other members of staff.

"Much obliged Miss" relieved that he would not have to report a complete blank in regard to Miss Standish to DI Crawford when he met him at lunchtime.

"Call me Irene," she extended a hand which Ted shook, "but not when Matron's around, she does not like familiarity."

"I'll try and remember that, although I doubt I will need to call again. I would love to stay and put one of those cups to use but I am afraid I've got other people to check off my list, so I will just have to bid you good day."

Ted had reached the door when he found a reason for delaying his parting from the delectable Irene. "Just one other thing, you would not happen to know who owns this place would you?"

"As a matter of fact," smiled Irene, happy to have a few more moments talking to the handsome visitor, I can. You see I'm the Secretary come Accountant for the Home, so it's not a case of nosiness but I have to issue the cheques to the shareholders. Not that there has been very much profit to distribute the last couple of years. Miss Standish is one and the only other ones are Doctor

Carrington and a couple of sisters, one of whom died just after Christmas."

"You, Miss Irene, are a treasure. I shall really be in the boss's good books having discovered all this. The lady who died it wasn't a Miss Henderson was it?"

"As a matter of fact, it was, but how….."

Before she could complete the sentence, Ted cut in "if you'd like to have a drink sometime, I will let you know, but for now I must dash. Goodbye It's been an absolute pleasure."

As he walked at a swift pace back to the junction of Lyddcastle's roads which met outside its only pub, Ted pondered on his behaviour and that of the lady he had met at the Nursing Home. Had he been indiscreet? Probably, but he doubted he had revealed anything he shouldn't. Had she been flirting with him? He rather hoped so, but he had useful information whatever the reason for acquiring it. An evening with Irene in the backrow of the Swanage or the Grand cinema was something to dream about but it seemed he had Miss Standish's whereabouts which was a concrete achievement of his morning's work.

When he arrived at the Hinton's Farm House, Ted was welcomed in by Mrs Hinton who, without asking if he wanted it or not, served the DC with a large mug of piping hot tea. "I'm glad you've come" she said, "In a way it shows what I've done hasn't been wasted, well not that it was a waste anyway, cos it's done what my husband said it would."

Bemused DC Egan enquired, "Which was?

"Settled my mind. I mean I take it's about poor old Miss Henderson you've come. Her dying like that was a proper shock and Albert said - write it down Doris, then you'll sort it in your mind and stop fretting."

"Would you mind letting me have a look at what you wrote?"

"Not at all," she beamed, and bustled out of the room leaving Ted to sip his hot tea, as he began to suspect he was going to have three successful visits out of three to report to his boss.

Returning, Mrs Hinton handed him two sheets of plain paper full of neat hand writing.

It read as follows:

I went to the church at about ten o'clock like I always do every couple of weeks in order to polish the church ornaments and make sure everything is neat and tidy. When I went in, I saw Miss Henderson by the font. I sort of thought she was bending over like she was having a drink, not that you would but I am trying to sort things in mind so I must write what I thought at the time. I got closer and called out hello but when she didn't respond I had an awful feeling something was wrong and went up to see what she was doing. When I saw the way she looked, I screamed out. Not that I thought she was dead but perhaps she'd had a stroke and I hadn't a clue what to do. Old Tom came in from outside and I saw the Vicar walking up the aisle. The Vicar, Mr O'Donnell, was very good he sort of took charge. He must have thought I was proper barmy cos I was gabbling about her being like one of Albert's lambs and just needing a slap but the Vicar seemed to know she was gone and laid her out real gentle like and put his mac over her. He sent Old Tom off to get Doctor Carrington and when they came back the Doctor confirmed what the Vicar said, and that she was dead and it was probably a heart attack. He is a kind man, the Doctor, and he seemed to want to take our minds off things and started to fuss over the Vicar's black eye. After he had left, the three of us agreed that we would all wait for the ambulance to come and collect her. The Vicar suggested we say some prayers and took out his glasses and prayer book. Now it's come to me. Albert was right. I realise why I was so upset. I reckon I knew that Miss Henderson was dead and I was just not wanting her to be dead, because the

45

last time we had met we had ill words. I can't remember what it was about, but I must have been trying to stop my mind thinking we had parted for the last time on bad terms. I feel much better now. The Vicar having sort of a service made me feel that her spirit was at peace with me. It was a lovely end and she could not have wished for a better ending, being in the church she loved, near her adored Vicar.

"Mrs Hinton, you are a marvel. Exactly what I wanted to know, all written down before I've had to ask one question."

"I'm pleased I could help. Writing it down was certainly a help to me, but it's done it's job in settling my mind, so you are welcome to keep it."

"I will if you don't mind Mrs Hinton. It will save a bit of paperwork."

By this time, the tea, on top of the coffees he had drunk with Oliver Henderson, was having an effect and, before leaving, Ted requested and was granted the use of "the facilities." Hence, in more ways than one, it was a relieved young man who made his way to keep his rendezvous with DCI Crawford.

Both men tucked in to their sandwiches as they shared the results of their morning's work. At first, it was Ted Egan who did most of the talking, while his DCI savoured his food. Afterwards, Crawford shared the results of his morning's work. Although it was not strictly necessary for a DI to do this, he valued other viewpoints and thoughts knowing the sharpest mind will sometimes miss something.

Pouring a couple of cups of coffee from the flask he had learnt to keep on hand for lengthy observations he reported not only on his visit to the Vicar but the post mortem report, which had been waiting on his desk at the police headquarters. "The Pathologist has no doubt that she was smothered to death. There were no drugs in her system other than a mild sedative, which matched the stuff in one of the bottles we found at her house. There were some fibres in the nostrils, which I very much suspect will match the cushions from the pews, but Sergeant Brownlow is going to get one of the cushions to see if we can get a match. One of the most surprising things is what turned up when they went through the dead lady's pockets. We found a handkerchief with the initials JO on. There's no suggestion that it was used to do the smothering as there was no saliva on it, but it seems odd that she should have found a handkerchief with the Vicar's initials on. There was very little sign of bruising so the suggestion is that either she was grabbed from behind or knew her attacker as she does not seem to have resisted. There were no traces of skin under the finger nails, as one might expect had she struggling but then an old lady would not be difficult to subdue, if taken by an adult man unexpectedly."

"The other thing I have done some research into while you have been doing the leg work is about the ownership of the Woodside Lodge Nursing Home. I am not sure if it will prove to be of any relevance, but I did some research about its ownership. Apparently, it was set up just after the war. According to Companies House, the original share capital was divided between three doctors by the names of Standish, McDermott and Henderson, plus a building firm. I am guessing this would give them some security for the building costs and that they would probably sell them when the project was up and running. From what Mr. Daltry told us, if anything, the Home is losing money, so it's not something you would think someone would murder for, but if one had control of over 50% of the shares you might make a packet from building on the land or selling it for some other purpose. Property in the village is highly sought after but, if my thinking is right, it's all irrelevant."

"Well, what is your theory Sir," asked Egan, "or would you rather not say at the moment?"

"On the contrary, I would like to share it with someone because the facts seem to tell me I can't be wrong, but my Copper's nose is telling me I am. Let's get out of the car and go for a walk, it will clear my head and I can explain." The two men got out of the car and began to walk along the stretch of open turf between the churchyard and the cliff edge.

Crawford never tired of walking on the Purbeck Cliffs. The chalk soil drained so you seldom got your shoes wet and the open land and skyline cleared his mind.

"First, I want to try a bit of logic on you. Let us begin with two facts. The first is this, that Miss Henderson was murdered inside the church between the time she entered it, just before nine o'clock and the time Mrs Hinton found her body. Do we have any evidence to contradict that factual statement?"

"None at all Sir, In fact quite the reverse, from what you tell me of the results of the post mortem."

"In that case, does it not follow that the murder could only have been committed by someone in the church at that time?"

"I can't disagree with that."

"In which case Constable you will be able to give me a list of suspects."

"Well, there's the Vicar" and at this point, Ted Egan stopped looking stunned, as his mind searched and failed for other names to add to the list.

"Exactly, so if our premises are correct, we have our murderer."

"Mm, if that is how the facts point, I would say the facts are wrong."

Turning and looking back along the way they had come, the Inspector tapped his nose, "Facts are never wrong if they are correct but it seems, like me, you have a copper's nose and something doesn't smell right. Let's get back to the car, there is something in that statement of Mrs. Hinton you gave me I want to check again."

The return walk was done rather quicker than the outward one, and once back in the car, Inspector Crawford began scanning through Mrs Hinton's statement.

"Well, I never," he exclaimed, "he's been lying."

"Who?", queried Ted, wondering who his colleague was talking about.

"The Vicar, you see he told me that he had come in to the main church and seen what we now know was Miss Henderson's body and thought she was still alive"

"I can't see anything dishonest in that, he wasn't to know was he."

"No it's not that. Let me finish. He said he had come out of the vestry to look at the Bible on the lectern because it had big print and he had forgotten his glasses yet, in this statement, Mrs Hinton says he took them out of his pocket!"

Inspector Crawford was clearly shocked at the knowledge that the Vicar seemed to be lying. "What I can't understand" he said "is why lie about that and not about the door to the Vestry being locked. It makes me even more confused. Why lie about one thing and not lie about something which could wreck my theory and could hardly ever be disproved? It makes no sense."

"I'm not quite sure I follow."

"All the evidence we have says that no one could have got in to the church without being seen. If the Vicar says the Vestry door was unlocked when he got there, or he did not lock it after him, the theory is blown out of the water."

Inspector Crawford saw he was in danger of sitting on the horns of a dilemma. Starting the car, he explained to Ted Egan the reason for the journey they were making. "We have been focusing on a financial motive and it's never wise to forget other possibilities."

"Such as."

"Good old fashion jealousy for one. The Vicar is evidently a much sought after chap. What if another lady parishioner was jealous of our Miss Henderson. When I first interviewed him, the Vicar mentioned a lady who bought him candle snuffers. I doubt she is involved, but we ought to check she has got an alibi for the sake of completeness, and it will give us a chance to get another person's take on Mr O'Donnell.

They found the lady concerned as soon as they had pulled up on the concrete area standing between a house and some stables. Janet Clayton emerged from the latter. She seemed a little wary, holding the pitch fork she had been using to muck out in a defensive posture across her chest. Before the two officers had taken out their warrant cards and had a chance to explain the reason behind their visit she spoke, "What's my Donald done now, not left his ruddy shot gun lying about again."

The conversation that followed established that the police were not interested in Donald's shot gun or any other of his possessions and it was the good lady herself they were interested in talking to. This information seemed to bring about a relaxation in her mood, and she invited them in to what appeared to be an office come kitchen. However it seemed she might have changed her mind, for she turned around blocking the doorway. Removing her own riding , she said "I'd be obliged if you would wipe your feet, there is enough muck in here already."

The state of the room in general and the sink with upturned mugs and brown stains made Crawford relieved that they were not offered tea or coffee.

She said that on the morning of Emily Henderson's death she had been mucking out and feeding the horses. Unfortunately, she had no one to confirm it as Donald now referred to as "that useless article", had gone off to the races at Salisbury and taken Katy, the stable girl, with him. The DCI assured her he had no reason to doubt her word, and that he wondered if she knew Miss Henderson and whether she knew anyone who might have had a grudge against her.

This opened a flood gate. Whether she had ever heard of the advice not to speak ill of the dead or just chose to ignore it she let rip. "Old termagent, I am not surprised somebody did her in. She could never mind her own business, self-righteous old bitch."

It came as quite a shock to the two officers hearing this about someone who had in death appeared to have achieved an almost Saint like reputation.

"I would not have thought you had much to do with Miss Henderson?" interrupted an increasingly interested Crawford.

"I didn't, but it's what I could have if she had not been like she was. I made it clear to Donald he would have to have someone here on a Sunday as I would always go to church and I did, despite her."

"In that case I can't see why you are so critical of her."

"She was a different type of Christian to me." Ted was beginning to suspect the Catholic Protestant divide was about to rear its ugly head.

"My parents taught me that if you were a Christian you did two things, you went to church and you helped the poor. She might have done the first, but not the second. Why only a couple of weeks ago, I suggested we should send some money out to Kenya to help the poor orphans, and she promised she would raise it at the next meeting, but I doubt that she did because no money has gone. She would be much more concerned with mending a couple of gargoyles or a crack in a stained glass window."

"But wouldn't such things be a matter for the Vicar?," asked Crawford.

"Yes but I was going to say he is just as bad, but that would be unfair. He is a good man basically, but inept and he was terrified of her. Whenever someone suggests giving money to the poor, she was so two faced. She would clutch the Vicar's arm and simper 'oh it's a lovely idea but do you really think we can afford it. We will have to get the Accounts up together and see what we can do.' Of course, that would have meant him doing some work and getting the Accounts straight. Don't get me wrong, I don't think he was fiddling the books or anything, he wouldn't have had the brains for it. I offered to help him do them same as I do for that financial illiterate Donald, but he always put me off and do you know why?"

"Sadly not," mused the DCI, "but hopefully you can tell us."

"Lord knows but I will tell you another thing. If he had got the books straight, she would have been on at him 'get some new hymn books,' mend the roof and, of course, that would have all been more work for him. He only needed to say how beautiful her flowers were and he spent so much time admiring them and he really must get round to doing the Accounts."

"Do you think the church authorities have any reason to be concerned."

"No, all he needs is a level headed woman. He is worth three of that Donald. A couple of weeks away from Miss Henderson and that wittering cleaning lady of his and I could sort him out. He always keeps himself smart and hands, he has got beautiful hands."

Feeling he had heard enough from this rather biased source, Crawford apologised that he had taken up too much of her valuable time already and along with Ted Egan returned to the car.

Attempting to part on a friendly note, Ted called back over his shoulder "I hope your husband comes back with a winner."

This was a mistake for it brought forth another volley of abuse "He's not my husband and I can't think of any sane woman who would marry him. No wonder you are just a PC, if you think I would marry a waster like that. I am his Estate Manager, that's what I do and that's what he calls me. Not that he pays me like I am. That Katy girl gets up one morning a week and I get up on six yet I don't get paid six times as much and she does not have to worry about sorting out the stupid old buzzard's accounts and court fines."

Quickly and speedily, Ted jumped in to the passenger seat and breathed a sigh of relief, as a smiling Crawford drove off. "Don't take it to heart but learn something. First lesson of police work never assume anything," he comforted the crest fallen DC. "I must admit I was thinking Donald was her husband. It's only their husbands that most women are so abusive about."

"I pity any man who married her," moaned Egan.

"Actually, you have revealed a piece of information I might well have missed. If she is not married but an Estate Manager, she might be fishing for a way out of early mornings and away from horse muck."

"Meaning she could have her sights on the Vicar?"

"It is a possibility."

"Poor devil"

"So, it would give her a motive and, also worth considering, it would give the Vicar one."

"Surely not," argued Egan, "half an hour of her would be enough to last a life time."

"Some men like women to take control. They do say it was the late Queen Mary who wore the trousers whoever wore the Crown, and look at the Duke of Windsor."

"Begging your pardon Sir, but that does not seem natural to me. Remind me only to go out with girls from the typing pool not the woman who wants to be a Chief Constable."

Not wanting to be distracted by too much thinking while driving Crawford waited until they were back in the car park in Swanage before discussing his dilemma. Having pulled on the hand brake and switched off the engine, he explained to his colleague.

"On the one hand we have strong circumstantial evidence that the Reverend O'Donnell may have committed murder. If I do nothing and another parishioner gets bumped off it's yours truly will get the blame. If I arrest him the whole village and possibly the whole Church of England will be baying for my blood. I'm not usually one for passing the buck, but on this occasion, I think it's above my pay scale so I'm going to speak to the Chief Constable. That cock up with the Christie fellow is still in people's minds. Another mess up and people's belief in the police could be destroyed."

"That's right enough Sir." The grief some of my mates have given me, it's like I had hung that poor bastard Evans myself."

Sensing his colleague's discomfort, Crawford, a kind if correct man, slapped his colleague on the knee and confided "But you know that is not true and so do I. That sort of thing, Ted, is well above your pay grade and I think this one is above mine. Is everything you told me about the interviews you have done, true?"

"Completely Sir, surely you don't doubt me?"

"Indeed, I don't, but I ask the question for two reasons. Firstly, what did I tell you was the first lesson of policing?"

"Assume nothing."

"So, I haven't. That's the first reason and the second is, if you are telling me the truth which I have no doubt you are, we can both sleep easy in our beds if I have referred the matter to the Chief Constable."

Inspector Crawford was as good as his word. A phone call from a call box and a brief conversation saw him carrying news back to Egan that they were both summoned to police headquarters for a meeting with the Chief Constable. The fact that the Chief Constable was aware what a hot potato this case could be, was shown by his making them later that same afternoon.

As Crawford drove them towards the police headquarters, he explained his feeling about circumstantial evidence to Ted who was feeling quite cheerful that he had been invited to join the meeting with his two superiors.

"From a police work point of view it's never quite satisfactory. It leaves you feeling you haven't done your job," said Crawford. "The classic example was Nodder back before the war."

"Didn't he murder a young girl?" queried Egan.

"So the Court found and in all probability they were right, but it's a bit like this case. Nodder was found guilty of child abduction, but as there was no body he was not charged with murder. Sometime later, when he was in jail serving time for the abduction, the girl's body was found and he was put on trial again for murder. The only real evidence was that he had been seen with the girl by a few people at the time she disappeared but as to eye witness or forensic evidence, there was nothing. He claimed he had been taking her to see a new born nephew, and had left her nearby, but the jury didn't buy it in either trial and he was hung."

"Begging your pardon Sir, but I don't quite see how it's like this case."

"Well, it's like this, we have no forensic evidence or any other type of evidence that John O'Donnell murdered Miss Henderson but, if he was the only person in the church when she died, it must have been him. Similarly, if Nodder was the only person seen in the company of the young girl, who else could have murdered her?"

"I think I get it now Sir. What you are saying is could a jury really doubt that, in both cases it could be anyone else?"

"Exactly," said the Inspector, as a set of traffic lights changed and they drove on.

"I guess that what could help the jury find a doubt in this case is they are dealing with a well- respected member of the community and not a convicted child abductor."

"That's true, but on the other hand there was the opportunity for nearly anyone in the vicinity of the girl's home to have committed the murder as she was seen in an open area in which anyone could have been, but on the evidence we have, one man, with a good motive, is the only person who was in a locked building, who else could have done it."

Chapter Nine

Handling a hot potato

Chief Constable Bassett welcomed the pair into his spacious office and getting up from behind his desk waved them to sit on a sofa at the other end of the room, while he joined them sitting opposite. Having served as a Squadron Leader during the War, while he took his new job seriously, he saw no reason not to enjoy the comforts of office, and valued the time to make considered decisions which you did not have when a Me 109 was on your tail. His Secretary bustled in with a tray of tea and when they were all settled he said. "Right Inspector, if I understand you correctly, you feel that this Reverend O'Donnell should be arrested for murder."

"That's right Sir. Although given all the circumstances I felt I should speak to you first."

"So you're basically asking me to lend my approval?"

"Exactly Sir."

"In that case, take me through what makes you think he did it. If you can give me a method, motive and opportunity I will back you, but I want to be able to be sure of the facts in case people start questioning me."

"Very well Sir. If I may, I will go through things with DC Egan, who has been involved with interviews, etc., but please feel free to come in if you have any questions. I will start with Motive.

"Would you agree that John O'Donnell, the Vicar, Oliver Henderson, the nephew and the owners of the Woodside Lodge Nursing Home, all given Miss Henderson's Will, have a strong financial motive for killing Miss Henderson?"

"I don't think anyone could disagree with that," confirmed Egan.

"Hang on, have you seen this Will?" interrupted the Chief Constable.

Crawford explained that they both had and added, the solicitor had informed them that he had been due to see Miss Henderson about changing her will just a couple of days after she had been killed, which had added to his suspicions.

"Interesting," nodded Bassett, "I can see why you are suspicious. Do carry on."

"Given our researches this morning it would seem that Miss Standish, who we think at the moment is part owner of the Nursing home, has an alibi, being on duty at the Nursing Home. Oliver Henderson was seen by D C Egan. He has an explanation, but is honest enough to admit that he could not get anyone to support it. The only member of the trio, who had an opportunity, being in the church at the time Miss Henderson was murdered, was the Vicar."

"I see where you are heading Sir, but would the Vicar have the ability?" It was Egan who felt he ought to be doing all he could to raise any flaws in the case.

"Good question young man," said the Chief Constable, "You seem to have motive and method, but you have jumped over the first requirement, Inspector. Was she poisoned? In which case, she could have been poisoned before she got to the church."

"Unfortunately, the Pathologist is convinced she was smothered or strangled. There were no traces of poison in the system. Knowing this, I have done a bit of digging into the Reverend O'Donnell's past. I would have been inclined to think all three people with a motive might have been physically strong enough, but not necessarily proficient to smother somebody. However, it turns out that, during the war, the Vicar spent some time away from the parish near a town called Highworth. It was where they trained units of local civilians to operate behind enemy lines in the aftermath of any invasion. If you knew how to kill a Nazi soldier silently and swiftly, an eighty five year old lady, would be no problem at all. That leaves us with opportunity. As you said yourself Sir, only somebody who was in the church at the same time as Miss Henderson could have done it. It looks like we have definitely ruled out Miss Standish and, although he has no corroboration, it looks like the nephew was still travelling down from Oxford and did not arrive until after the murder had been committed."

The Chief eased himself back in his chair and smiled ruefully. "I can see why you are worried, but you have certainly done your homework and I would have thought there are certainly enough grounds for anyone to believe that a committal hearing would find that there is a case to answer. Can I suggest we send DC Egan off with our authority to get a search warrant for the Vicarage, and that you interview the Reverend O'Donnell, under caution, once you have completed the search. If at the end of the interview you are satisfied the facts you have outlined still hold good, then you have my backing to place him under arrest and we will bring him before the Courts. The decision, if he is guilty of murder or not, will be one for the jury to decide, but it shows the constabulary is doing its duty without fear or favour."

"With your permission then Sir, can DC Egan get off to a magistrate and apply for the search warrant?"

"Certainly, do you need me for anything else?"

"No Sir, you have been most helpful," and with that the two plain clothes men rose and took their leave.

As they descended the staircase, Ray Crawford said "If you take the car to get the warrant and bring it back here, I am going to get a squad car to take me to the Vicarage. I want to get on and arrest the Vicar, then I'll see what he has to say tomorrow. I want you to see if you can get some confirmation of the alibis of the other beneficiaries of Miss Henderson's will. Given we are relying **on** circumstantial evidence he, being the only person who could be seen benefitting by Miss Henderson's death who does not have an alibi, does not prove his guilt but it makes the case stronger."

I need to get the Case Record Book written up and tomorrow we can tackle things with a clear mind. I want to work out how I question our Mr O'Donnell without making myself likely to eternal damnation."

Chapter Ten

Crawford makes an arrest

It was nine o'clock when Crawford knocked on the door of the Vicarage. It was opened by the Vicar himself.

"Good morning, Sir, can we come in?"

Before he had received an answer, Crawford had gone past him and was walking down the corridor into the room where his previous interview with the Vicar had taken place. The Vicar, who had no intention of denying entry to the police, turned and followed while Ted Egan, clutching the unneeded warrant which could have gained them entry, brought up the rear.

"It might be best if you sit down Sir."

John O'Donnell did as he was directed taking a seat on the Captain's Chair. Ted Egan was full of admiration for his DCI. At police college he had heard tales of how you only got high rank in the police force by knowing the right people or having the right handshake. Here was a man who gave a lie to that story. Without resort to the Search Warrant obtained from the Chief Constable and showing consideration for the accused, he had taken control. Now, standing over the seated figure with its head bent and hands clasped, he uttered the words which every police officer was obliged to use "John O'Donnell, I am arresting you on suspicion of the murder of Miss Emily Henderson. You are not obliged to say anything but anything, you do say will be taken down and may be given in evidence."

Egan, who had been warned by Crawford to note down anything said, at first seemed to have an easy task, for the Vicar uttered only two words "Thank you."

After a brief pause he continued, sounding more like a Catholic penitent than a man who had just been charged with murder. "I am afraid that is where you are wrong Inspector, do sit down gentlemen."

Egan glanced at Crawford and, seeing him nod, he seated himself on the sofa where the DCI immediately joined him.

"My calling obliged me to bear witness to the Christian faith and all of its tenets. I knew you were coming - praying last night something in my head told me you were coming. It is strange. When poor Emily died, I was writing a sermon on the Ten Commandments. What the good book does not say is when you are entitled to break them. Thou shalt not kill - but David slew Goliath and was allowed to become ruler of Israel. Given my calling, I must not bear false witness at least not to benefit myself. So let me tell you Inspector, to the very best of my knowledge I may be responsible for her death, but I did not kill her."

"Thank you for your honesty, Sir. Can I ask you, therefore, are you sure the Vestry Door was shut and locked when you arrived?"

The Vicar who had been looking thoroughly miserable lent back and a wistful smile broke across his face "Alas I am, though it may send me to the gallows. My faith obliges me to tell you it was. It was shut and, being a Yale lock it had to be locked."

Again, although given his warrant he had no need to do so, Crawford asked if the Vicar had any objection to his property being searched. O'Donnell shook his head but said nothing. Ted Egan was despatched to look around but, in truth, Crawford did not expect him to find much. There was no murder weapon and no expectation of blood-soaked clothes or evidence of a clean-up operation. When he did return all Egan carried was a sizeable cardboard box, full of cards and letters, that he thought might be worthy of closer inspection. DCI Crawford agreed and indicated to the hunched figure of O'Connell that they would be taken away, but that Constable Egan would give him a receipt for them.

By now the Vicar was looking a totally broken man. "Do as you must, but I can't see how poking through a priest's private correspondence with his parishioners can help you."

"Have you got any Account Books?" asked Crawford.

"Sadly not, I'm not very good on paperwork. The Parish Committee do all that sort of thing. You'd have to ask Mr Daltry or Miss Henderson," realising his error he corrected himself, "but then of course you can't - Mr Daltry is your best hope. He was the Treasurer."

If Crawford had been puzzled before this interview it had done nothing to make him clearer in his mind as to what had happened in St Anselm's Church the previous Friday morning. The vicar was either an innocent man or a consummate actor but he had no idea which. Guilty men usually maintained a stony silence when questioned and demanded a lawyer. Innocent ones, given a loophole would immediately jump at the opportunity to say, at the very least, they were not sure about something indicating they could be innocent.

Although he had arrested the Vicar and would have every right to compel him to come to the police station, he preferred to give the Vicar the chance to do so of his own free will and asked, "Would you have any objection to coming to the police station to put what you have said in to a statement?"

The Vicar seemed only too ready to do so, saying, "Most certainly, now if you are ready, I think I am. I would like to get out of here before Mrs Mansion arrives."

Agreeing there was no purpose to be served by delay, the three men left the Vicarage and made to the police car on the drive. The Vicar was not to have his wish though, for, as they walked down it, Mrs Mannion came up it. Her appearance seemed to cause the Vicar to bear up or at least to try and put a brave face on things.

"Good morning, Mrs Mannion. I am just going to see if I can help these two policemen, so I won't be needing any lunch." Ted Egan was about to push the Vicar's head down as he got in to the car, but decided it was not necessary, as the prisoner jumped and ducked in one move into the back seat of the car. Crawford joined him on the back seat and as Egan drove off, his prisoner called out through the window "Mrs Mannion - please tell Miss Clayton that I have been unavoidably detained." Before slumping back on the seat of the car.

Mrs Mannion gazed after the car. Her opinion of the police had never been high, now it sank even lower. Fancy, she thought needing a man of the cloth to solve their problems for them and, being so inconsiderate, to take him away in such haste, when she had a lovely piece of haddock lined up for his lunch.

The Vicar was destined not to have the haddock on that day or at any time as having made the statement as requested Crawford had decided to charge him which meant he would be held in custody until he could be brought before the local magistrates.

Whether deliberately as a result of some sub conscious impulse, the bundle of letters taken from the Vicarage had remained unread. Egan had offered to take them home to read through them but Crawford declined his offer with thanks pointing out that, now they had charged Mr O'Donnell they could not question him further. Crawford did however take them home himself to read. He tried to convince himself it was a duty he should undertake but knowing in his heart there was an element of curiosity in his decision.

Most of the letters were of thanks for conducting a service or had evidently accompanied a gift, often of a candle snuffer but a series of letters from Clayton particularly attracted his attention and he read through them carefully in the order they had been dated

August 1952

Dear Sir,

I felt I had to write to say what a wonderful Sermon you gave on Sunday. Nobody had explained the conundrum of God permitting evil as well as you did in this sermon. It has almost made me a believer again. My parents preached but to my mind did not practice Christianity, which rather turned me against the church but meeting you at the races the other day, convinced me to come to your church. I must confess, it was the thought of seeing you again as much as your religion that made me come. Please find a small token of thanks in the form of a candle snuffer which a lady in the congregation told me you collect.

September 1952

Dear Mr O'Donnell,

Thank you for your kind letter of thanks and invitation. I will gladly accept but as long as you realise I am a feeble creature seeking enlightenment, not as you describe me an attractive young lady. I place one condition on my acceptance. I know you are not a Catholic but will you take my confession?

October 1952

Dear Vicar,

Thank you for your understanding. Hearing of your journey to your present position was illuminating and has made me respect you even more. That you refused to accept something you did not believe in to give you an easy life but still to show such respects for the tenants of the Catholic Church is, to me, true Christianity. I had no ill effects from the first of the three acts of penance you gave me by the next day, completed the second that evening and the third will find its way to your church funds.

November 1952

Dear John,

Thank you for your help with my second confession. I realise you were uncomfortable with it. I now feel capable of dealing with all three sections of self-confession and repentance that you feel should be the way of a true Protestant.

Whereas all the above had ended 'Yours sincerely' and been signed there followed a card which read simply, To John from Janet, hope you like the candle snuffer.

The final letter Crawford read and would given the Vicar's habit of keeping letters in order of receipt seem to have been given the Vicar's habit of keeping letters in order of receipt, was of a very different tone and nature and was undated.

Dearest Jonny

If that poisonous witch, Henderson is a problem leave it to me. Sending her to kingdom come with a blast from one of Donald's shot guns would be no problem and I can easily make it look like an accident. I am guessing I will have to do it as you are not man enough, hiding behind quotes from the Bible.

There was only one letter from Miss Henderson. It began,

Dear Vicar,

I have spoken to Mr Daltry about Miss Clayton's suggestion. While the lady herself is I suspect, no better than she should be the idea of helping the orphans is not without merit. I have asked Mr Daltry to come to dinner so that we can discuss his belief that somebody has been withdrawing money in a fraudulent way or that Mr Wilkins has been over claiming on his expenses. Once we have sorted that out, we can take the suggestion of Miss Clayton to the Parish Committee. I have to say that my own recommendation will be that the defects in the church (listed below), be rectified first but any surplus could then be given to the orphans or any other charity the Committee sees fit to favour. Does not the good book tell us we should not heap up treasures on earth?

Church defects

1. Damage to Madonna and child statue
2. Leaking roof above the altar
3. Threadbare carpets

Your sister in Christ

Emily Henderson

It all left Inspector Crawford, a kind but honest man, feeling he wished he had not read them. As far as the Vicar's case was concerned, there was a point suggesting he had a motive like taking money from the church funds, but a point in his favour by way of the words of Miss Clayton. Should he bring it to the attention of the prosecuting team or not? He decided being tired and not wanting to make a hasty decision he would sleep on the matter.

Awaking the next morning, it was Miss Clayton's position which determined his decision. He well remembered the fate of Edith Thompson hanged for indiscreet remarks in a series of letters. John O'Donnell had been charged and would be brought before the courts no charge had been brought against Miss Clayton and he did not intend to. What people write in letters and what they do are different matters and anyway Emily Henderson had not been shot she had been suffocated. He decided given that anything else in the letters could be testified to by witnesses, he decided to put the letters back in the store of evidence marked unused material.

Chapter Eleven

What have we done?

Bad news, especially if a bit of scandal may be involved, spreads quickly.

Thursday was half day closing in the Swanage area but by Friday morning a placard outside the Village shop proclaimed '**Local Vicar arrested.**' Having bought the local paper and read the article to which the headline referred, Nurse Mackenzie was devastated and enraged in equal measure. It required all her innate professionalism to keep her mind on her patients during the morning, and lunch time found her with little appetite as she picked at her home made salad. By the end of the afternoon, she was feeling no better and, by the end of her afternoon visits, she was seething with anger that such a good and kindly man should have been arrested. It was a feeling not helped by the realisation, that the careless conversation of herself and her fellow bell ringers had brought the Vicar's incarceration about.

Normally, she would have changed out of her uniform before going out socially, and would not have dreamed of going into a pub without knowing people she knew would be there. "Hell!", she thought, slamming the car door shut as she left it outside her house, what do I care if someone thinks a woman in uniform would not go in to a pub unescorted. Times are changing. Nobody would have thought of arresting a clergyman unless they had been caught red handed, would they? Despite her determination, it was with no little relief that on entering the bar she saw Sergeant Brownlow seated on his own. Like the gentlemen he was, he immediately rose and asked if she would like a drink.

"Actually, if you don't mind, I would rather have a double whisky." She had decided if it meant making an exhibition of herself to show the strength of her feelings, about the treatment of the Vicar, she was happy to do so.

Having acquired the neat double whisky, Sergeant Brownlow placed it before her and resumed his seat. "You are clearly not your usual self," said the Sergeant. After a brief pause giving time for a response which did not produce one, he continued, "I guess it's the business with the Vicar. I wondered, after what I have done whether you would still be talking to me."

This finally produced a response. "What you have done! It's what we have done. Had we bell ringers not sat gassing like a load of old washer women, casting aspersions and carrying on like we were trying to make up some murder mystery, when poor old Miss Henderson had just had a heart attack."

"But that's just it, isn't it. She did not die of a heart attack. She was murdered."

Nurse Mackenzie took a sip from her whisky and as the neat liquid burnt the back of her throat wondered why she had asked for such a foul tasting drink. "That's as maybe, but can you really believe that our Vicar did it?"

"No, but Inspector Crawford is not a man to go locking people up without good grounds."

"Well, can't you at least talk to him to find out what those grounds are?"

"I could but I doubt I will be too popular. It would seem like I was interfering and trying to trade on an old friendship."

"So," said the Nurse, "if this Inspector is as fair a man as you say he is, he won't mind explaining his reasons. Besides, if it had not been for your phone call a murderer would be escaping justice. Surely another phone call, to satisfy yourself that he has got the right man, is justified."

"Put like that I suppose it would be fair enough, provided I was tactful about it."

Having received an assurance by her fellow bell ringer that he would contact the Inspector as soon as he got home Moira Mackenzie turned to discussing other possible killers, while she and her companion finished their drinks. Having got the co-operation of the Sergeant over the phone call she informed him that she had the following afternoon off and intended to devote it to conducting her own investigation into Miss Henderson's demise. She was not sure she informed him of how she would do it, but she was sure she had no way of enjoying an afternoon off or turning her mind to anything else, until she had found the real killer.

Knowing that Moira Mackenzie would never countenance the possibility that the Vicar, a man he himself had always thought highly of, could be the real killer, George Brownlow kept his thoughts to himself but as he made his way home, he tried to decide exactly what he would say when he made his phone call.

Anxious to get it over with and not wanting to dwell on the problem over his evening meal the Sergeant, having greeted his wife, picked up the phone. As the ringing tone sounded, he rehearsed in his mind what he would say, which would largely be along the lines that while he himself would not have done it as he knew that his old colleague must have good reason for believing the Vicar did it his friend had been insistent.

It was something of a relief that Inspector Crawford seemed pleased to hear his voice and less worried about any reason for the phone call. It was even more of a surprise when the Inspector said "I can guess why you are ringing."

"You can?"

"It's about your Vicar friend."

"How on earth?" started the Sergeant before he was interrupted by his colleague...

"It would be a poor detective who could not deduce why someone he had not heard from for months should ring twice in a matter of days about unconnected issues. Nor does it take the brain of a Sherlock Holmes to deduce that you are unhappy about the arrest of your Vicar. To be frank I am not happy about it myself."

"Well Sir, I would not have presumed, but a fellow bell ringer was most insistent and said you would not be affronted."

"Actually, it might have saved me a phone call. How would you feel if I got you taken off your normal duties to assist me for a couple of days or so?"

Pleasantly surprised at the way the conversation was panning out the Sergeant was only too happy to try to co-operate. "Only too glad if you think I can help but not too sure how I can. After all, am I not a bit compromised having such a good opinion of the Vicar?"

"That's why you will be ideal for the job I have in mind. I'm no Catholic, but I have always thought that when somebody is considered for Sainthood, they have a devil's advocate to find anything that can be said against them. By the same token for me, it's only fair that an accused man should have somebody making sure anything that can be said or any evidence that can be found should be before the Court. Many officers might just go through the motions, but I know you will do a conscientious job and take nothing for granted. Would you be willing for me to get you seconded to me for a week?"

When Brownlow had signified that he was more than willing Roger Crawford promised he would organize a replacement for the following week at his station and for George Brownlow to join him. George explained he was rostered for a free day but would be more than willing to forgo his day off and get started as soon as possible. Hence, he was invited to attend an interview which Crawford had arranged with Miss Standish for Monday morning and he readily agreed.

Sergeant Brownlow was more than glad to have made the phone call before his evening meal. He ate it with more relish than he had expected, and was soon relaxing in his armchair opposite his wife, whose knitting needles were clicking away in the chair opposite, looking forward to his next week's work more than he had for a long time.

Chapter Twelve

Nurse Mackenzie Investigates

On Friday morning, Nurse Mackenzie having finished her morning calls, went to visit Cliff Top House. She had no trouble in obtaining the keys from across the road, explaining that she wanted to check no pills or medicines had left behind. In truth, she guessed the police would have gathered them in their inspection, but made a point of checking thoroughly for any they had missed, so that her visit was not a complete deception. She spent time looking carefully around each room in turn. Any drawers that were opened had their contents surveyed and then tidily closed. By the time she had finished the second room, she was desperately thinking what she was actually looking for. Beyond the fact that she would look for anything pertaining to why Emily Henderson had died, she thought she would also look for anything that might raise a question mark about her sister's death, but, beyond this, she had no idea what it might be. Neither lady's bedroom seemed to yield anything of interest and by the time she had been round the house she was beginning to feel intensely frustrated. Perhaps, she thought, she should have known better. Sergeant Brownlow had told her what a competent officer Inspector Crawford was. Highly likely then that if there was something of relevance, he would have found it. She slumped down in an armchair, wondering if there was anything else she could do to help the now imprisoned Vicar. Her eyes roamed over the wall full of books in the room in which she was sitting. So many had lettering on the spine but something seemed to draw her eye to a thin plain green one. She got up and placing her finger on top of it gently withdrew it. As soon as she saw the handwritten wording on the front Diary of Emily Henderson 1953, her heart leapt. Hardly able to contain herself, she flicked over the pages with her thumb. The final entry had been made on the 16th April, the day before her death. Tempted to read this straight away she recalled the words of old Doctor McDermott, that if you wanted to treat a patient, don't just read what the Doctor had recorded from the last visit, read the case notes from the start. Pushing the book into her case, she rose and left the building closing the door firmly behind her and dropping the keys back through the letter box of the lady who had given them to her.

Driving home, she wondered whether she should hand the diary over to the police. Her conscience told her she should but, given the police had had the opportunity to take it and hadn't, she could see no reason why there was anything wrong with her reading it first. The next morning she would hand it over to Sergeant Brownlow, whatever its contents.

Arriving home, she made herself a large mug of coffee and settled down to read beginning with the entry for the 1st January, which read as follows: A New Year but I cannot say a happy one. It is the first since my dear sister has not been at home to see it in with me. Her own decision means that she is now resident in the Nursing Home. I have always thought it a nice enough place and my father's participation in it a good act of Christian charity. It was I thought though for other people, not for family. My sister's condition when I last visited her is in no way improved from when I last saw her. I am resolved that I will die in my own bed here at Cliff Top. May the Lord give me strength to refuse food and water when that time comes, that my earthly suffering may end and I may, as dear John says, "join the faithful and not so faithful."

The entry for January 2nd saw Emily on an entirely different track, worrying about her garden. I have spent today putting seeds in seeding trays and arranging them in the greenhouse so that they will catch what little sun we have at this time of year. I must remind Thomas that he can always fill his time with a bit of watering in the greenhouse now the grass does not need cutting so often.

The following day saw Emily back on the topic of her sister and concerns about the Nursing Home. When I arrived at Woodside today it was just like old times. For half an hour I chatted away with my sister and she was her old argumentative self. Then it was like a switch had been turned off and she fell in to a deep slumber. I suspect it is what they put in the drink. If one or two of the residents need medication to sedate them, I would not put it past that Matron to give it to them all willy-nilly. They offered me a drink, which I suppose was kind, but I would not touch it with a barge pole.

Reading on, Nurse Mackenzie was amazed how, whether dealing with her own daily doings, national events, or the dying of the light on her sister's life, all was recorded in the same neat well-rounded hand. She felt sure, if she was patient and read it carefully, some light would be shed on anything untoward about Emily's death. Sure enough, an entry for the 2nd April got her attention and showed she was on the right track.

I am resolved that I must make a new will. Saying the Lord's Prayer at Holy Communion made me aware I have a problem. It contains the words "thy will be done." The problem I have now is that, having inherited my sister's money, I must in all conscience consider what she would have wanted to happen to it. She had always been a great supporter of the Nursing Home. Indeed, she had often said she would like to see me share any money I inherited from her with it. Silly girl that she was, she never made a will, saying that was an indication you wanted to die. Now the solicitors are making hay, getting probate etc etc. It will all come to me eventually, but apart from being able to live in this house, I really have no desire for it. In all conscience, I should leave anything I got from my sister to the Nursing Home but, God forgive me for saying so, I think they hastened her death. It seems an awful thing to believe and rather illogical, as they would be far better off keeping patients alive or so I would have thought.,

I spoke to our dear Vicar this morning. I had managed to persuade him to take me back to the Vicarage on the pretence of looking at the garden to see if there were any flowers I could use for the church. Having arrived, and while standing looking at the flower beds of the Rectory Garden, I broached my problem and my thoughts about the need for a new will. Well, honestly, he was no use at all. He began by saying that on no account was I to leave him any money, the Lord had granted him sufficient for his needs and there were far more deserving cases when my death, which he hoped was far distant, required me to divest myself of my earthly treasures. Beyond this, he would say nothing, apart from a suggestion that I should consider saying a brief prayer for guidance, when I got home, and letting the bible fall open at a certain page and point to a spot within it.

Today's service offered no further enlightenment. Walking home and feeling it could do no harm, I decided to follow the Vicar's advice. I can see why he gave it. He is so clever with words that he could twist anything to say what he wanted, but I was not so naïve as to believe a random pointing at a page would pick a nugget of wisdom, so I followed John's suggestion in so far as praying and letting the bible open to a page at chance, but resolved to read the whole page. Having made a brief silent prayer that I might be guided by his will not mine, I let the Bible fall open. The first heading of the page, which was part of the Book of Ecclesiastes was Chapter 17, and it was from there I began to read. When I reached Verse 16 it hit me like a wet flannel in the face. "Be not too righteous." Who was the Lord talking to, me or the Vicar? On consideration, I felt it had to be me. John is, more than one of his congregation have suggested, far too forgiving rather than far too righteous. It was I who was being too righteous. My initial thought was confirmed by the words that followed: "Do not make yourself too wise." Was I not, in believing my sister had been poisoned, making myself too wise? I had to admit I had no medical training and perhaps grief was warping my view. Then followed five words which left me marvelling at the ways of the Lord and convinced me that in our Vicar we had a man of rare truth and innocence. "Why should you destroy yourself?" Had my sister killed herself and if so why?

Am I rambling, possibly so, but one of the reasons I keep this diary is in order to reflect on my thoughts so if they ramble so must I record them.

The following day I awoke having slept better than for some time and went to my sister's bedroom and said a brief prayer for her soul and our reunification. The Sun was shining and it seemed clear to me that I had to rewrite my will, but not for the sake of revenge, but with good will to all men and women. I would see that my sister's share of things in regard to the Nursing Home was carried out as she would have wished. For myself, I feel I need to mend some bridges with my nephew. So I will invite him down, to ask his forgiveness for scolding him at times. It must have been awful to lose your mother at such a young age and in such a random chance way. I do not think it would be amiss to remind him of the parable of the talents but will reassure him that I will provide the talents to use as he will.

Nurse Mackenzie was reading these words with somewhat mixed feelings. While she felt increasingly sad that such a kind old lady should have met her end by foul means, she was no nearer finding a reason for anyone to carry it out. While there was no indication of anyone losing out under the will, there was the additional problem that nobody knew what Emily had intended. Feeling she would need something to make her sleep, with her mind being in such a turmoil, she resorted to the bottle of whisky she kept for Christmas and medicinal purposes and, having poured herself a hefty double, she read on.

Only a couple of pages remained to read, when she came across something she thought had a key importance, as it explained the reason for Emily being in the church when she was. It read as follows.

Delightful news today, Oliver rang. He is going to come down next Friday to see me. Apparently, he is in some theatrical performance this week but will come down next. I will bake a cake and put raspberries on the top as I know they are his favourite. He is intending to get here about eleven, so I told him I would go to the church earlier than I normally do and make sure I was back at Cliff Top to meet him. I am so glad he is coming. I did wonder if I was a bit harsh in my letter. Those words about not being too righteous are so true. Even when he mentioned a theatrical performance, I was mentally thinking he is going to grow up to be a waster like his mother. But there I go again, thinking evil of people. He is my brother's son, and if we have had an on off relationship, he can be very kind at times. His letters seem to be showing the benefit of an Oxford education and I will be telling him that I am going to increase the share of my estate I intend to leave him. Do you know I feel better already. Our Vicar is such a wise man. I do believe, if he was a Catholic, they would make him a saint before he had been dead long.

This begged the question, "If the nephew was getting more who was getting less?" If it was the Vicar, would not that be a motive and make things look even worse for him? There was no indication as to any other changes of beneficiary, or that she had told anyone else about her intended will changes before she died.

It was a heavy-hearted nurse who went to her bed that evening. Her faith had never been strong, although the sermons of John O'Donnell had done much to strengthen it. If it turned out he was after all a murderer, she would question her very existence and secondly if there was any point in her work, which often involved prolonging suffering before painless oblivion. One thing possibly innate, possibly imbued in her by her parents, was an obligation to tell the truth. For good or ill, she would share what she had found with Sergeant Brownlow.

With this in mind, and an idea that had come in to her head about how she would spend the next day, she rang Sergeant Brownlow and asked if he was free the next day, would he like to join her on a trip to Oxford to see if they could speak to Oliver Henderson, the nephew of Miss Henderson. With his wife away at her sisters, he had been intending to spend some time on his allotment but given his coming secondment and the reason for it he felt it was an offer he could not refuse.

Chapter Thirteen

A trip to the Dreaming Spires

Having met up outside the church at half past eight, by nine o'clock Nurse Henderson's Morris Traveller was making good progress through Wareham, and by eleven thirty, they were approaching Oxford by what, had they been locals was known as the Abingdon Road. Somewhere, just before Newbury, Nurse MacKenzie realised that, apart from the name of the nephew and his college, they had not got any reason for wanting to speak to him, and apart from saying she suspected him of murdering his Aunt, which probably was not true anyway. Would this put him on his guard and probably ensure they learnt nothing of value if so they had no reason for speaking to him or for coming to Oxford. When she confided this point to the Sergeant, her grip on the steering wheel tightened with frustration and her eyes began to mist with tears.

Pondering for a few moments, the Sergeant began to smile "Can I suggest something?"

"I wish you would."

"If, as a fellow bell ringer you discovered I was coming to Oxford to see an old friend, might it not be quite understandable that, as a good friend of Miss Henderson, you thought you would kill two birds with one stone and give me a lift and take the opportunity to see her nephew to extend your condolences."

Thus, it was, having parked just off the main road and walked back up to it they found a hostelry where they partook of a coffee and a sausage roll and refined their plan. It was agreed that Brownlow would try to contact a fellow officer who had been with him at Hendon and that Nurse MacDonald was going to do some sight-seeing. Given that Christ Church was on the same side of Oxford and just a little further up the road, the pair decided to leave the car where it was and walk up to the college. Nurse MacKenzie had brought her Box Brownie camera to add realism to their story. Of course, everything depended on Henderson being in and their gaining access to him and at first it seemed they had been successful on the first point, but not the second. A small wooden door within a much larger closed one gained them admittance and to their left a bowler hatted figure, behind a small counter and in front of a board lined with keys, asked if he could help.

Having explained the reason for their visit and the name of the person they wished to visit the man in the bowler confirmed they were in the right place. He gave them the number of Oliver Henderson's Room and directed them to it with a warning he had no idea "if the young gentleman is at home."

Thanking him, they were about to follow the directions indicated when he called after them. "One other thing."

Turning as one, they were relieved that all he said was "Please take care not to walk on the grass. That is a privilege reserved for fellows."

Relieved, Sergeant Brownlow ensured him they wouldn't and proceeded on their way.

Having climbed the stone stairs and knocked on the number of the room they had been directed to, there was no answer and they were disconsolately considering their next option, when the door next to it opened and a tall, young man emerged. "Looking for Oliver?" he asked.

When they confirmed this was the case, he smiled and added "You have probably timed it well. He is off playing squash, silly game if you ask me, ball is too small and your opponent is behind you half the time, but he should be back any minute."

Relieved they had hardly got past exchanging names than a red-faced figure with a towel round his neck and clutching a racket, came towards them.

"These two are looking for you" said the tall young man and then, turning to Brownlow and Nurse Mackenzie added "Afraid I must love you and leave you, got a session booked in down the Bod." With these words he took his leave, leaving Oliver Henderson to his visitors.

"What causes me to be honoured with the presence of such a lovely lady and so distinguished a gentleman?"

As agreed, Nurse Mackenzie explained how she had come up to Oxford with her fellow bell ringer to give him a lift to see his friend and before doing some sight-seeing wanted to express her condolences to him on the loss of his Aunt.

"That's jolly considerate of you, I must say. Were you leaving this young lady to her own devices?"

The question was clearly directed at Brownlow and when he nodded adding "Just for a couple of hours."

This caused Oliver Henderson's eyes to light up. "Could not possibly allow a charming mademoiselle to walk the streets of Oxford unaccompanied. Allow me to be your guide on a sight-seeing tour."

Realising this would give her the perfect opportunity to find out a bit more about Oliver and his relationship with his Aunt, Nurse Mackenzie readily agreed. Oliver enquired if they would wait for him to change down in the quad and this gave the pair the chance to confer, before he joined them some fifteen minutes later. It. was agreed Brownlow would come back to the college main gate at five thirty and that Nurse Mackenzie and her escort would rejoin him there.

"You certainly picked a nice day for it," beamed Oliver and as the spring sunshine beamed down on them it would have been hard to disagree. Oliver led the way up the gentle rise to the Town Hall on the corner outside it directing her attention to Tom Tower on the opposite side of the road. He was an engaging young fellow she thought, and between pointing out the sites, asked her about how long she had been a nurse and did she have Scottish ancestry. She allowed the conversation to focus on her thinking this would help build up his confidence and encourage him to speak more honestly. Oliver pointed out the beauties of Oriel College before turning down a road that led them down a side road that took them past the circular Bodelian Library.

"Old Dawlish is in there swotting away, still he's not a bad old stick."

Seeing the chance to move the conversation towards her escort she broke in "Did you know him before you came to Oxford?"

"No, we chanced to be roomed next to each other and signed up for the OUDS together. I think he takes life a bit more seriously than I do, but he still finds time to do some acting and he is a dam sight better than me on remembering his lines."

Discussion of the abilities of some other thespians continued until they entered Balliol College, where it was suggested they have some refreshments. "A pot of tea or something stronger?"

Having indicated that tea would be fine to her host, she found when the waiter brought out a large pot of tea, he had added an order for a couple of scones. "Finest scones in Oxford. Dig in and see if you can disagree."

While acknowledging her experience of Oxford cuisine was limited, she agreed they were delicious before confiding in him that she actually had another motive for speaking to him, besides giving her condolences.

He smiled, "To have one reason for meeting such a lovely lady would be fortunate, to have two is a sheer delight. Do tell me"

"It's our Vicar. I expect you have heard he has been arrested for your Aunt's murder. I can't believe he would murder anyone and I wondered if you might be able to shed any more light on things."

"I can't say I know much about the Vicar, but I am sorry to say I was rather glad to hear he had been arrested. You see, I was rather afraid the finger might be pointed at me what with Aunt Emily having left me money and me having no alibi. I managed to ply the young PC who interviewed me with enough coffee and he seemed reasonably content, although he asked if there was any way I could back up what I said."

"What had you said?"

"Let me think. I started by telling him how I had arranged to meet my Aunt at eleven o'clock at Cliff Top House, that's where she lived. I told him I had left Oxford about seven and stopped for a breakfast somewhere between Newbury and Ringwood, it was on the left-hand side of the road if I remember rightly. When I got to Cliff Top the door was open and I went in and shouted upstairs - there was no reply. So I checked the upstairs rooms were empty and then asked a neighbour. She said Miss Henderson nearly always went to the church on a Friday morning but usually later than the time she had left that morning."

"So the Vicar wouldn't have expected her to be in the church at that time?"

"Not if what the neighbour was saying was true and I can't see why she would lie. She must have changed her routine because she was seeing me." Suddenly his eyebrows lifted, "Cripes if she hadn't arranged to meet me she might still be alive." His head sank in to his hands.

Putting a hand on his shoulder, Nurse Mackenzie comforted him "You can't blame yourself. The only person who is responsible for her murder is the person who did it."

"I am sorry about your Vicar. I'm sure he is not responsible, but I just wish I could find some proof that there was no way I could have been anywhere near the church when she died. You see it does look devilishly suspicious, me being a major beneficiary and her intending to change her will."

"Were there were other beneficiaries besides you and the Vicar?"

"So the solicitor chappy said."

"Was one of them a Doctor?"

"Not that I can recall but I think a nursing home was mentioned when the will was read to us."

"I only ask because it seems the local doctor got the cause of death wrong."

"That's true, but if every Doctor who got a diagnosis wrong were hung for murder the medical profession would very soon become depleted."

Oliver Henderson refilled their cups, "Let's change the subject. It's far too nice an afternoon to talk about sordid things like murder. My Aunt's in a better place, but this garden is a pretty nice one anyway and is enriched by your beauty. Let's enjoy the day while we may, it will be gone all too soon."

The Nurse agreed, pointing out they only had some forty minutes before they were due outside the Christ Church gates. Her companion agreed but, pointing out it would take no more than quarter of an hour, he suggested she tell him something about bell ringing in the time remaining to them. After she had explained about the numbers required for a full peal and a little of the history of bell ringing, he seemed mesmerised and then broke in. "Sounds a lot better than Am Dram, perhaps I should give it a go some time."

He signalled for the bill and, when it was delivered, took out some papers along with his wallet from his sports jacket. One of the papers fell to the ground and he applauded as the Nurse caught it. She was about to return it, when she saw the name on the top of the paper.

"Is this the place you stopped on the way down to your Aunt?"

"By Jove. So it is, and the dates on it."

"Doesn't that prove you couldn't have murdered your Aunt?"

"I suppose in a way it does, but your policemen friends will say I could have got that anytime of the day that my Aunt was murdered. You see it doesn't have a time on does it."

"That's true, it's just got a table no, a date, bacon and eggs, coffee, amount due and a squiggle, which I presume is the waiters."

"Holy mackerel, that's it, or rather bacon and eggs is."

"What are you on about?"

"The bacon and eggs, they only serve them until ten so I must have been there in the morning and could not possibly have got to Lyddcastle to murder my Aunt. You'd better take it and give it to that policemen friend of yours."

The Nurse agreed she would and, while pleased that Oliver Henderson had got evidence to ease his worries, was soon reflecting that all her visit to Oxford had achieved was to eliminate a possible alternative suspect and made the Vicar's position no better.

The realisation that this seemed to have been the only result of their day's efforts, meant the return journey began in a rather subdued mood. As she drove, Brownlow related how he had spent his afternoon. He was somewhat apologetic that he could not find something more directly related to the purpose of their trip but had managed to visit the Playhouse and picked up some leaflets, which gave him a bit more information about the OUDS. There was nothing in it that did not tally with what Oliver or his companion had told him about their involvement with it.

Brownlow continued "I must admit that after that, I treated myself to a pot of tea and a scone in the Randolph. It was very pleasant and not as expensive as I had feared. It actually proved quite a stroke of fortune, as a smartly dressed chap with a bow tie saw me looking at the literature about the OUDS. He asked about my interest and I was able to steer the conversation to the two guys from Christ Church. The cast are always identified by their college you see, and it was quite interesting what he had to say about the two we met today. He dismissed the friend as just going along for the ride and to enjoy the post show parties, but our Miss Henderson's nephew seems to be a bit of a problem."

"In what way? He was quite charming with me."

"Oh, nothing bad, just a problem regarding casting. They all agree he is a great actor, but hopeless at remembering his lines. It meant they could not really put him in a major role, which they felt his ability deserved"

"How come the chap knew all this?"

"He is a Don, and apparently a patron of the Society - Hob nobs with the director and cast."

"All very interesting, but I am not sure it helps us at all," sighed the Nurse. "Are you in any hurry to get back?

"No, the wife's gone to her sister's so it does not matter when I get back."

"The thing is I would like to stop at this place where the nephew had his meal. Just to check a couple of things out."

"Let's do it. I need to spend a penny after all that tea in the Randolph."

Hence it was, that a short while later, they pulled in to the car park of The Barrington House Hotel. They ordered sandwiches and a pot of coffee for two and sat in the lounge. Under the guise of visiting the convenience, Brownlow was able to look in the restaurant which contained about a dozen tables. When the waiter delivered their order, the Nurse thanked him and asked if he was on duty on Friday mornings. He confirmed he was but, when shown the bill that Oliver Henderson had given Moira, said it must have been done by somebody else.

"This is not my handwriting."

"So you would not have changed that 11 to a 17 where it says date. Only we are anxious to confirm on which day it was done," said Brownlow. "the 17th was a Friday so the 11th must have been a Saturday."

"In that case I will tell you it can't have been the 11th. You see the initials MW that is Mrs Watkins and she does not work on Saturdays."

The pair ate their sandwiches and Brownlow was aware that Moira seemed very depressed that their trip to Oxford had done nothing to help the Vicar's case and, if anything had made the case against him stronger by giving an alibi to a possible suspect. Sensing this, and anxious to cheer his companion up, he said. "I think there is one avenue we could pursue and that's the Nursing Home. Not that I am suggesting the Doctor or Miss Standish would murder anyone, but it's on a prime piece of real estate and there are some unscrupulous people about. You only have to look at what happened in the Blitz, people taking rings off dead bodies that were buried in the rubble of their own houses. We might think we live in a nice civilized part of the country, but you never know when someone might come in and think they can exploit people's good nature and naivety."

Sadly, Moira was forced to agree and, while she did not give voice to the thought, was conscious that sometimes even the nicest people had a dark secret. Could that be the case with the Vicar?

When they arrive back outside the Sergeant's house in Lyddcastle, Nurse Mackenzie asked her companion to wait a moment. Going to the boot of the car she took out the diary she had found and handed it over with an apology for not confiding in him sooner. George Brownlow pulled a bit of a face but said nothing apart from warning her he would have to hand it over to DCI Crawford on Monday. I know we are seeing someone in the morning but it might be worth coming in after lunch and you could explain how you got it. He got out of the car but before Moira drove off he turned and said "Mind you given tomorrow is Sunday, and I am seconded to him next week I can't see any harm in not taking it in until Monday. I can read through it tomorrow and if you want a chat pop round tomorrow evening and we can reflect on what's in it and what we found out today."

Chapter Fourteen

Reflections on the diary.

As invited Nurse Mackenzie arrived at George Brownlow's house on the Sunday evening. She received a warm welcome from George's wife, Mary, and was soon seated in the parlour. Moira was confronted by tea and lemon drizzle cake and the instruction to have as much as she wanted, but to see George only had one slice. When they began to discuss the diary, Moira was rather depressed. She thanked George for coming with her the previous day, but felt all they had done was to make the outlook against the Vicar look stronger.

"You are surmising too much", stressed the Sergeant. "As I see it the only two facts this diary gives us are, the reason Emily was in the church earlier than was her normal habit, and that her nephew was going to benefit from the new will."

"Yes, but you would hardly kill someone before they changed their will to give you more money and we do not know if Emily had told the Vicar that she was going to cut him out or reduce his share in the will."

"I am not going to argue about that but, equally, we do not know if she had told anyone else that they were going to lose out under the new will. We do know though, that John told Emily not to leave him money. He would hardly murder her to stop her doing what he asked. Would he?"

"That's true. I hadn't thought of that. So, in a way it's a point in his favour. Now you say in most ways we are only surmising and I may be reading too much in to it. What about Emily's bit, about being too harsh in what she wrote to the nephew. Is it just my female intuition saying there is something more to his getting in touch, and agreeing to come down here."

Brownlow stroked his chin and considered for a moment. "More likely a case of a chap aware where his bread was going to be buttered and making sure he kept it that way. Still, perhaps we should try and have a word with him, or at least find out if the Inspector thinks he needs closer investigation and get him to follow it up."

Chapter Fifteen

The Matron's Confession

The first task of George Brownlow's secondment was to sit in on an interview which DCI Crawford had arranged with Miss Standish, the matron of Woodside Lodge. His official brief was to help in gathering information in the case of miss Henderson's murder but Crawford had told him to leave gathering the evidence for the prosecution to him while he was to concentrate on anything which might throw suspicion on persons other than John O'Donnell. As far as the interview of Miss Standish was concerned, he had been asked to make any notes he wanted and to chip in with any questions, before Crawford brought the interview to an end.

Having been told by Crawford, when he invited her to come in for interview, that he was seeking her co-operation as a witness, he had expected her to come alone. It was with some surprise therefore that, when she presented herself at the front desk of the police headquarters she was accompanied. The Desk Sergeant assumed the person with her was a solicitor but in fact it was Doctor Carrington.

Sitting in one of the more salubrious interview rooms and with the introductions having been made, Miss Standish seemed anxious to speak. "First Inspector, I have to apologise if you have been misled. When your colleague came to Woodside he was given to understand that I was actually working on the morning of Miss

Henderson's murder. Given it had not involved me telling a lie, I had been content to let this misapprehension remain but with the vicar being arrested and charged, I cannot in all conscience fail to tell you of where I was that morning, although hopefully the details of what I was doing are of no import.

"I am afraid I will have to be the judge of that. A woman has been killed and I need to know everything that may be relevant," warned the DCI.

Looking distinctly uncomfortable, Miss Standish bit her lower lip but, before she could speak, Doctor Carrington broke in, "I think you had better let me explain. We have nothing to be ashamed of. We are both adults and are of opposite sexes and neither of us is married." Having addressed these comments to Miss Standish, he turned to face Roger Crawford and continued "On the morning in question, Miss Standish was at my house that is why I was I was able to respond to the phone call so quickly. I was in bed with this lady and, I can assure you, that is a far pleasanter way of spending the time than going out murdering old ladies."

"Thank you for your frankness, Doctor. Given your honesty, I don't think what you have told us need go beyond these four walls and I can assure you the Medical Council will hear nothing from us."

"Medical Council be blowed you can tell them and whoever else you like. I may be the Doctor for the Nursing Home residents but this lady has her own Doctor in Swanage."

Miss Standish had now begun to weep and the handkerchief which had been used to fumble with was now employed to stem the flow of tears.

"Do stop crying dear, Lord knows we have both seen enough pain and suffering to last a couple of life times. Why should we not find a little comfort in each other's embrace." As if to show the truth of his words he wrapped his arms around her.

"I shouldn't have arranged for a swap and not put it on the Rota but I had such a bad week last week with one of our resident's dying and trying to sort out the Bank overdraft. I needed to get away and I knew Doctor Carrington is only to glad for me to come round and he is such a comfort."

Seeing the evident distress of the lady who seemingly had nothing to be ashamed of Sergeant Brownlow interjected, "I can't see any harm in what you have done, can you Sir?"

"Indeed not," confirmed the Inspector," but there are a couple of things you could help us with, if you feel up to it."

These words seemed to restore something of the composure you would have expected from a matron to Miss Standish and she announced herself willing to do her best.

"The first point may be one you can both help us with. Miss Henderson's sister, as you will both know, died at Woodside Lodge around last Christmas. I will be frank, we have been told that Miss Henderson seems to have blamed you for her sister's death. Can you throw any light on it?"

It was a somewhat disgusted Doctor Carrington who broke in, "We are both well aware of that and you can rest assured that it's absolute rubbish. Her health had been failing quite rapidly which was the reason she went in. Unfortunately, she had suffered a series of infections and her whole system was packing up. For God's sake she was ninety two!"

"Calm down Peter, grief takes people in funny ways. With Emily it was feeling she had to find someone to blame."

"I dare say both of you are right," reassured DCI Crawford, "but I have to ask – do either of you consider there was any possibility she was murdered?"

It was Miss Standish who answered. "Absolutely not. I should know. I never left her bedside during the last six hours of her life. Thankfully she would have been blissfully unaware of it but I could tell the end was near, that's why I stayed. The breathing becoming more laboured and then that horrid rattle in the throat. No matter how many times you witness it, it never gets any better."

Anxious not to cause the Matron of Woodside Lodge any more distress, Crawford moved on to his last point. "I understand you are the Matron but who is the owner of the Nursing Home?"

"I own a quarter of it, although if it wasn't for my Matron's salary, I would not make much out of it. The rest is a little complicated so let me explain. Back in the twenties there were two Doctors here and the surgery served Lyddcastle and Studland. They thought a Nursing Home would benefit their patients as well as being something of a money maker. Funds were getting tight in the early thirties but thanks to the generosity of the church which gave the land and the builders who took shares in the business they managed to get it up and running. The church was very generous as they though it would benefit their parishioners so they gave the land under some sort of Covenant so it cost nothing. Everything looked fine until Doctor McDermott died and that could have wrecked the whole enterprise had it not been for Major Henderson. He had just retired from the Army Medical Corps and agreed to take on Doctor McDermott's share. He was the brother of the Henderson sisters and, after that, things went extremely well. We seldom had any spare beds and, I know it's awful to say this, but war casualties proved an absolute boon.   Well off families were only too pleased to pay for their sons to be accommodated here while they recovered. When Peter – I mean Dr Carrington joined the practice, he paid to buy the builder's shares. He was a replacement for my father when he died you see."

"I take it that your father was one of the original Doctors and you inherited his share and became a part owner. Or did you buy them?" asked Crawford.

"They were my father's shares and came to me on his death about ten years ago. I was Matron by then but his death left us a Doctor short. Doctor Carrington was looking to move down from London and buying the builder's share solved two problems.

"Look," said Doctor Carrington who was beginning to look increasingly annoyed, "If you are suggesting this lady has murdered a couple of old women to get control of the Nursing home you are barking up the wrong tree. The Henderson sisters have nothing to do with her share. Since that blasted National Health Service was introduced the home is losing money hand over fist. It's six months since I was last paid!".

"Calm down dear." Look Inspector, even with both the Henderson sisters dead, there is no way the shares in the nursing home are of any value. Under the Covenant by which the Church gave us the land, it can only be used with the agreement of all the shareholders and the Church Council. Nothing can happen until the Henderson sisters' estates are settled as Major Henderson divided all his shares equally between the two sisters even then I doubt the church would agree."

"Well thank you for all that Miss Standish. And thank you Doctor for coming with her, you have obviously been a great support. I don't think Sergeant Brownlow and myself need detain you any further."

After Miss Standish and Doctor Carrington had left, Crawford turned and asked his colleague. "What do you make of that?"

"I suppose, from the point of view of the investigation, the most important thing is that each of them gives the other an alibi, although given what Miss Standish says, they don't actually need one as neither of them benefits from Emily Henderson's death."

"I agree with you on the first point but I am not a hundred per cent sure on the second. Before our victim was murdered, in the church who would be the holder of all the Major's shares?"

"Why, Emily Henderson and she could queer the pitch of any sale or facilitate it if she was so minded." Slowly Brownlow was beginning to see where the Inspector was coming from. "So, what you are saying Sir is that if she knew that Emily Henderson was intending to change her, and what was in it, she might have felt it worth killing her before she could change it. Would that make Miss Standish a suspect?"

"Technically yes, but I don't think a very likely one. For one thing strangulation is not a woman's murder method. For another, I don't think her conscience would let her be a murderer. She was in a complete state about admitting to having sex outside of marriage. I can't see a person who cares so much about that being a very likely murderer. Finally, we have convinced ourselves that the church doors were locked with only the Vicar and the victim inside. Besides, to get in she would need to have access to a key and where would that have come from?

That afternoon, at following Brownlow's suggestion Nurse Mackenzie came to the police station and, the pair met Inspector Crawford and his colleague and handed over the diary. Crawford raised his eyes and shook his head "You do realise this is evidence and should have been handed over straight away. However, given you informed Sergeant Brownlow, who I have asked to be involved with the case, I suppose there is no great harm done." Nurse felt he was making it clear she was an amateur and should be aware of interfering too much but in a not unkindly way, and relationships between them were in no way damaged.

The Inspector took charge and continued, "I think Sergeant Brownlow, it would help if we went through our suspects one by one and you told us how you think the diary strengthens or weakens the case against them. You may remain Nurse, but only because I feel you may have knowledge that may help our investigations. Please, remember you are here as a witness not an investigator."

Turning to the Sergeant he said "Let us start with the Vicar, "Is there anything in the diary that indicates that he had arranged to meet Miss Henderson in the church?"

"No" responded, his Sergeant.

"Is there anything in the diary that indicates that Miss Henderson intended to remove or reduce her bequest to him?"

"No," was again the response of the Sergeant.

"In which case, I think it neither strengthens or weakens the case against him. It says nothing about any other way of getting in or out of the church. He was the only person in there at the time and, apart from the deceased herself, the only person who had a key. However strong a motive anyone else may have had if they were not in the church and had no way of getting into the church, they could not have done it."

Nurse Macdonald could contain herself no longer. "What if someone got in the church during the bell ringing practice and concealed themselves?"

"A fair point and perhaps justification of my asking you to remain as a witness. Constable, would you like to ask this good lady the obvious question."

PC Egan, momentarily shaken, asked "Did you see anyone?"

"No," responded the Nurse, somewhat crestfallen.

"And you Sergeant?" interjected Crawford.

"No Sir."

"Still, we are looking through people with possible motives. What about the nephew? You certainly seem to have uncovered him as having a possible motive. Any views Constable when you interviewed him."

"Well Sir, he certainly seems a bit odd. Very dramatic. Seems to be acting a part all the time, but I don't see him as a murderer."

"Appearances can be deceptive. If I did not think that I would not have arrested the Vicar. Having spoken to Miss Henderson's solicitor, if I did think anyone other than the Vicar had a motive, it would be the Matron of the Nursing Home. She seemed distinctly uncomfortable when she came in to admit her relationship with the Doctor and if Miss Henderson had lived long enough to change her will, she would have stood to lose out big time."

"Not if what we found in the diary was true," broke in Brownlow.

"That is as maybe, but Miss Standish, or Doctor Carrington come to that, knew what she intended to do. For all they knew she was still intent on bringing the medical authorities down on Woodside like a ton of bricks."

Nurse Mackenzie felt she had to intervene as a fellow member of the female sex. "Inspector, what you have to realise is that for a lady of her age, in her position and dealing with people of the age she does, to have any involvement with a man who was not her husband, would be frowned upon at the very least."

Inspector Crawford slumped back in his chair. He was a patient man, but Nurse Mackenzie was beginning to try him and he finally voiced his frustration. "You seem to want to prove the Vicar is innocent, yet every time I suggest someone else might be responsible, you pour cold water on it."

"I know Inspector, and I'm sorry, but I wouldn't want to clear the Vicar by putting another innocent person in his place."

"Well, that is highly commendable, but I have enough faith in the jury system to believe if there is a possibility that the Vicar was not responsible, at least one of the twelve jury members will give him the benefit of the doubt. As far as I am concerned, I am not going to spend any more police time chasing red herrings. How you and the Sergeant spend your free time is up to you, but I think we are finished with you. Are we not Constable?"

Egan nodded in agreement and, taking the hint Nurse Mackenzie rose pushed her chair under the table and, thanking the officers for their time, left. A nod from the Sergeant received an unspoken consent to leave from Crawford, and he rose and followed the retreating figure of the Nurse.

Outside sat in a car together, the Nurse let her head sink on her chest. She really thought she had been getting somewhere with the discovery of the diary, but now it all seemed to be leading nowhere.

Outside, she turned to George and said, "Do you think the Vicar is guilty?"

"No, but policemen are not always right."

"Exactly, and I am not prepared to rely on a jury if I can possibly help it. Besides, even if he is found innocent, whoever did kill Miss Henderson should not be allowed to get away with it. I intend to make sure that does not happen."

Chapter Sixteen

An interesting discovery

The following day, Nurse Mackenzie was at home. Being a District Nurse meant that she had a phone in her house. She thought it might be a patient when it rang, but it turned out to be Geoff Brownlow. When he said he had an interesting piece of news, she invited him to come round and some twenty minutes later, she was pouring tea and listening with interest to the tale that George unfolded.

Having cautioned her not to get her hopes up he added that it was something that the police investigation had not turned up. "I tried a friend in the Planning Department and would you believe an application has been put in to knockdown the Nursing Home and build three houses, which the application termed spacious, executive style residences. The application is from a building company who are making it on spec as it were. Evidently, it's conditional on the present owners being willing to sell and the planning permission being granted. It would certainly give the current owners a very nice windfall. I am going to have a go at getting the name of the building company and trying to find out how it has come about they are making the application. I rather guess they won't be to forth coming though. Another thing I turned up was that the Nursing Home land and the Church itself are part of a five hundred year lease, dating back to the reign of

Henry the Eighth. Apparently, the land belonged to a monastery, although the church was there already."

"I'm surprised it was not knocked down then," observed Moira, remembering the dissolution of the monasteries from her Tudor and Stuart School history.

"The Abbot of this monastery seems to have been a bit smarter than the Glastonbury chap who ended up getting strung up top of the Tor. This Abbot, apparently, gifted the land in return for a personal pension."

Moira snorted "Typical, line your own nest and who cares about the ordinary monks?"

"That's as may be but the way this chap worked it the church itself came out alright. All the land was to pass to Henry the Eighth's male heir on their twenty first birthday."

"Don't tell me," insisted Moira, and, after a brief pause for thought, exclaimed "Edward VI!"

"The very same."

"But didn't he die while he was still a teenager or was that Edward V?"

"They both did."

"So, what happened to the land?"

"That is where the old Abbot was so clever. Until the King's 'male heir' reached his majority, it was to remain in the care of the church. What better protection than looking after it for the King's heir."

"King's male heir! Given they were sexist even then I guess Ann and Elizabeth never got a look in?"

"True."

"Much as I enjoy bringing back school room memories, I don't see what help it is, or even what relevance it has, to trying to find out who suffocated poor old Miss Henderson."

"Neither did I when I got home. Then, when I was eating a second helping of the wife's jam roly poly, I remembered what I thought was just verbiage and so would most people."

"Which was?"

"In the event of the King's male heir not reaching twenty one, the ownership reverted to the church in perpetuity and then came the words the importance of which only hit me as I enjoyed the last scrapings of custard - 'in perpetuity" and "so long as the church officers bare true allegiance", that bit does not matter but the bit that follows does, 'be of good conduct and uphold the King's peace. What clearer breach of this peace is there than murdering a woman in your own church!"

Needing time to think, Moira got up and reached down two small glasses and a bottle of whisky which, as a Nurse, she would have assured you was for purely medicinal purposes. "George, I think you deserve a drink. Let's just have a two minute silence to think and enjoy and then I am going to ask you a question."

George gladly complied, having enjoyed a first smoky taste of whisky he saw the label Llaphroaig on the bottle and made a mental note to buy a bottle himself.

"Don't think I am not grateful. You have done well, but I am not sure I see how this helps us, although I think it might."

"I tend to agree," sighed George, adding on a more helpful note "but if the Vicar was convicted, as I read it, all this land reverts to the Crown. The church might object to the land being commercially developed, but the Crown would not."

"Then it is just possible that a firm or individual with a vested interest might be willing to murder and frame to make money."

"To make an awful lot of money, I agree, though it's a long shot." Regretfully, knowing a second glass of Llaphroaig would be his for the asking, but aware his wife would be beginning to worry, the Sergeant lifted himself up and begged to be excused.

An interesting discovery

Moira showed him to the door and opened it. Before he was allowed to leave, she grabbed his sleeve and kissed his cheek. "Bless you George, you are such a good man." Sheepishly he thanked her for her hospitality and hurried home.

Chapter Seventeen

The Committal Hearing

If it was a cricketer Swanage Town Hall would have been Trevor Bailey in that it could turn its hand to several different functions and perform them all well. Hence it was not only the Town Hall but the Magistrates Court, with a stage platform for the magistrates and a mobile witness box that could be wheeled in or out as occasion demanded. It was here that the Reverend O'Donnell was brought from the Police Station just across the road for his Committal Hearing. The day of the hearing was chilly and the showers forecast on the wireless had turned in to be a fairly continuous light rain. Although she was supposed to be working, Nurse Mackenzie had persuaded a colleague who wanted a long weekend later in the year, to do a swap and attended. At first, she had intended just to lend moral support but, after much deliberation, she thought she might be able to help in a more positive fashion. In order to do so, however, she would need to make contact with the Reverend O'Donnell's legal representative and as she walked to the Courthouse, she was aware she had no idea who it was.

In fact, the Vicar's legal representation was provided by the Church. It could hardly be said the diocese had pushed the boat out as, although the representative was a qualified barrister, he was very inexperienced and was sent down from London, as the experienced man of whom he was a pupil, had no wish to make the journey, when more lucrative work was available in London.

Sat on a narrow wooden bench in the foyer of the Court, Nurse Mackenzie identified two men, clad in dark jackets and pin striped trousers, they had to be the legal representatives of the Crown and prisoner. One was a plump self-satisfied looking man of about fifty, the other, a taller thin man, was glancing around furtively. Whether this was because he hoped or feared he would catch somebody's eye was impossible to tell.

Nurse Mackenzie opted for the latter for her first shot. "Excuse me, are you representing Mr O'Donnell?"

There seemed to be a mixture of terror, that somebody knew what he was doing, and joy, that somebody was interested when he responded. "Yes, do you know him?"

"Not personally, but I am one of his parishioners. A bell ringer at his Church actually."

"Oh, you are not a witness, are you?"

"No, but I do believe the Vicar is innocent and I think I have something that may be off interest and could help you. If you could spare me ten minutes."

"We are likely to be called on in a few minutes, so I can hardly do it now, but if you would like to meet in the luncheon interval?"

"That would be fine. There is a cafe down the road, shall we meet there?

The consent of the barrister was interrupted by a Court Usher calling all involved in the case of the Crown v O,Donnell into court. Having found a seat that was no less narrow and uncomfortable than the bench in the foyer, Nurse Mackenzie settled to watch the morning's proceedings.

Given the proceedings were expected to last all day and would have meant the normal Court business would have been delayed, a separate Bench of Magistrates had been called in. It consisted of an elderly gentleman with a military bearing and two ladies, both wearing hats and one with a lorgnette, which she flourished in ostentatious manner every so often.

The Magistrates' Clerk asked for the prisoner to be brought up and a trio appeared in the dock consisting of two prison wardens flanking the Vicar of St Anselm's, alias the prisoner. The prisoner's head was bent and he held his hands clasped in front of him in an attitude of prayer. He retained this posture as he confirmed his name and address. It was only when the charge "that he did wilfully and with malice aforethought murder Emily Henderson. How do you plead?" that his posture changed.

Raising his head, he spoke in a strong clear voice. "Not guilty, on my honour, and if you will give me a Bible, I will happily swear upon it." Having finished speaking he fixed the Chair of the Bench with a steely eye.

The aforesaid Chair seemed momentarily speechless, but was rescued by his Clerk who said, "Thank you Mr O'Donnell, that won't be necessary just yet. Mr Canford, can you outline the case for the Crown? The Clerk to the Justices intervened thus sparing the Chair, who was doing a passable impression of a carp with indigestion.

While most police prosecutions in the magistrates' courts were conducted by Police Inspectors, for major cases the local solicitors engaged counsel for the police. Hence a barrister with chambers in Bournemouth had been employed for this case. Hence, as the clerk had requested it was Mr Canford who began to explain the events of the Friday morning on which Emily Henderson died. If Moira did not warm to him she could scarcely say he was anything but scrupulously fair, although the number of the times he used the word "we" did become rather repetitive. The only point at which he was anything but matter of fact was when he concluded, "I submit that, like Sherlock Holmes, having eliminated the impossible whatever remains, however improbable, must be the truth." With this, he ostentatiously swept his gown behind him and said, "I would like to call Detective Inspector Crawford.

The Inspector, clad in a dark grey suit mounted the witness stand and took the oath. Not the least of the attributes of a man destined to go as far up the police hierarchy as he chose was his manner of giving evidence. He spoke clearly and confidently and, having carefully studied his police note book before the hearing, had no need to refer to it. Perhaps his greatest strength was that he never over stated his case and therefore, did not find himself having to go back on what he had said previously and spark doubts in a juror that, he really did know what he was talking about.

Defence Council was intelligent enough to realise this, but felt he had to say something to justify his presence. Knowing Crawford hadn't, he felt safe in asking "You did not mention any forensic evidence?

"No Sir."

"So, there was no forensic evidence?"

"No Sir," the Officer interjected, "There was forensic evidence. Traces of the fabric from the pew cushions were found in the victim's nostrils and on the hands of the defendant but, given he and other witnesses have given evidence to the effect that he had handled the pew cushions in a perfectly innocent fashion, I did not think it fair to mention it."

"No further questions." With this, the young barrister sank back on to his seat. The first time he had opened his mouth in a capital case and he had been left feeling they may well have helped contribute to sending his client to trial if, not yet, the gallows.

The evidence of the pathologist who had conducted the post mortem contained many long words and much medical terminology, but boiled down to the fact that Emily Henderson had been murdered. As to by whom, apart from the fact that it was somebody sufficiently strong to overpower a small eighty five year old lady, his evidence did little to enlighten.

Chastened by his brief questioning of the previous witness, Mr Redpath, the young barrister sent down by his Pupil Master declined to cross examine and the Chair of the Bench announced lunch would be taken.

Not knowing the locality, the aforementioned Mr Redpath was only too willing to accept Nurse Mackenzie's suggestion that they have their lunch at a sea front cafe. It was early season and outside a spiteful wind was blowing. The former meant they had little problem in finding a window seat where they would not be overheard, while the latter helped explain why, independently, they both opted for tomatoe soup and a crusty role for their mid-day repast.

"You must think me an awful dunce. I walked right into letting the policeman chap get in about the stuff on the Vicar's hands."

Sympathising, Moira tried to reassure him. "Nonsense, he did say there were perfectly reasonable ways he should have traces of cushions from his own church pews on his hands."

"I felt I had to do something. I came prepared to make a bail application, but Mr O'Donnell wouldn't have it, muttered something about "blessed are you when men shall persecute you.""

Little did Mr Redpath realise how much these words wounded the lady sitting opposite him. She was beginning to feel her Vicar almost wanted to be found guilty, as though it would be some kind of justified punishment for some wrong doing - surely not murder. Digging in her handbag, she brought out a sheet of paper and turning it round slid it across the table. Seeing the look of puzzlement on his face she explained. "Looking at numbers carefully is something we were taught at medical college. Make sure you are reading them correctly - doses, numbers of tablets to be taken and how often. Otherwise, I would not have noticed it.".

Redpath studied the paper she showed him. Still bemused, he said "I still don't see what is it?"

"Read the date."

Next to the printed word date were the hand written figures *17/4/53.*

"Look at the seven," insisted Moira.

"Now you mention it that does look a bit odd. I would expect the seven to slope but it is very upright. Now I look at it the colour looks slightly different.."

"It just seems too much of a coincidence. This was given to me by Miss Henderson's nephew. You will notice it is a bill for bacon and eggs which is only served up until ten o'clock. This nephew had assumed it would not give him an alibi, as he could have got it any time of day. Then, he suddenly realised that as bacon and eggs were only served until ten o'clock, it gave him an alibi. What if he got the bill on the previous Saturday and changed it to Friday?"

"It would certainly seem very suspicious."

"Do you think you could use it?"

"I'm not sure, I would have to put it to him. Can I hang on to it?"

"I was supposed to have handed it to the police, but seeing as I haven't so far, another few hours will not make a difference.".

"Well, he is not due to give evidence until tomorrow, but I could hand it to the police before I go back to London."

"I can't think there is anything wrong with that. If you tell them I asked you to give it to them it can hardly be said I was concealing evidence.".

"Quite so, mind you I am not promising I will put it to him. I will have to wait and see what he says in evidence. I may think it better to keep my powder dry as it were, until I hear what he says in evidence. It may be better to hold the information about your suspicions until a trial. The Magistrates are only concerned about enough evidence for a reasonable case, not a reasonable doubt that it might have been another person who committed the crime".

"I see your point. To be honest I don't see Mr Henderson as a murderer but I am damn sure the Vicar isn't."

Ronnie Redpath was quite awe struck with the vehemence with which these words were uttered and responded by saying, "Rest assured I will do my best, but if my advocacy was half as convincing as yours, I am sure the Vicar will be taking Sunday services again soon."

On this note they parted, although not before Nurse Mackenzie had scribbled her phone number on the bill which Ronnie insisted on paying, claiming he could put it on expenses and asked the young barrister to be sure to let her know how things went the following day.

That evening as she sipped her evening Horlicks Nurse Mackenzie, for the first time in many years, wondered if being a District Nurse was what she wanted from life. It was not that she did not enjoy the job, but it tied her and meant she would not be able to give at least moral support to the man charged with defending her Vicar. She had worked hard throughout her education, to be able to support herself and not depend on a man. To have to change your name and give up your career to bare his children had always seemed a most unequal bargain. Now, within a week, she had met two men who, on first sight were people she could happily live with. One would, she thought, be more fun and the other a better father, but both might free her from tending the sick to living a more adventurous and care free life.

Another person considering their future that evening was Ronnie Redpath. His parents had been more than generous in supporting him through a public school education, which he hated, and qualifying to be a barrister which he loved, but time was surely running out with his father due to retire in a couple of years' time.

These thoughts passed through his head as it lay on a pillow in the Victoria Hotel. The hotel took its name from the Queen of that name who had stayed here with her mother the Duchess of Kent. It was scarcely worthy of the price it charged and Ronnie would have felt more comfortable in a bed and breakfast with a small room and a large breakfast but his Head of Chambers had reminded him that the name of the firm, required he stayed at the best.

The next morning saw the solicitor bell ringer called as the first witness of the day. Knowing the solicitor, Mr Canford, the Prosecuting barrister, knew the only mistake in flattering him would be in not laying it on with a trowel.

Mr Daltry," he began, "Is it true you were Miss Henderson's solicitor?"

"It is."

"And is it also true that you had asked to be divested of this honour?"

"It is."

"Can you inform us of why you wished to be relieved of this duty?"

"You may. You see, while neither myself or the late Miss Henderson had any pecuniary interest in common, I did feel our positions as Church Wardens might be seen as creating a conflict of interest. I have always believed in the maxim that justice must not only be done, it must be seen to be done."

Canford turned to the Bench before asking, "Then might I respectfully enquire why you retained the position?"

"You may." At this point he looked pointedly to the Bench. "Miss Henderson insisted on my retaining the position. Myself and my father had looked after the family's affairs for years and she would not hear of anyone else handling it."

"Consequently, if their Worships looked in your diary, they would find that she had booked an appointment with you on the Tuesday after her death."

"They would," confirmed the solicitor.

"Are you able to tell us the reason why she had made this appointment?"

"To a degree, she had informed my Secretary that she wished to alter her will, but as to what changes these were she had not said."

"So, if anyone knew they were a beneficiary under the content of the existing Will, and knew she was intending to change it, it could be seen as a motive."

"Indeed it could," confirmed the solicitor.

"To your knowledge, had Miss Henderson communicated the content of her will to anyone."

Archibald Daltry looked down as if undecided whether to speak or not, and then his Head came up and he began to speak, "Unfortunately she had, most inappropriately in my opinion, she used to joke with the Reverend O'Donnell about leaving him money to buy sherbet lemons. I know the amount he would receive under the will is a very sizeable bequest and totally inappropriate." The word inappropriate was being used repeatedly and, looking at the solicitor's face, one might have thought he would have preferred to have said the wages of sin had he not feared being ridiculed.

"Apart from the defendant, were you aware of any other beneficiaries who had been informed?"

"She may have done but I was not aware of it, if indeed she did."

At this point, the Canford indicated he had no further questions and sat down, Then the Bench then enquired if Mr. Redpath had any questions.

Feeling the sooner the witness left the box the better it would be for his client, Ronnie rose and resumed his seat in one movement, accompanied by a "No questions."

The Chair of the Bench thanked the solicitor, who seemed anxious to leave the courtroom as quickly as possible, and his place in the witness box was taken by a very different figure. That of Oliver Henderson.

He upset the Chair of the Bench by responding to the Usher's reading of the oath.

"Absolutely," but once this had been apologised for and the correct response made, his evidence went smoothly. All he was able to do was to say how he had arranged to visit his Aunt over the phone at eleven o'clock and found her absent when he arrived at the agreed time. He was very frank in saying that it was concern over her talking about changing her will, that had brought him down from Oxford to, in his words, to keep the old girl sweet.

Perhaps, sensing this witness might be willing to implicate another suspect, the prosecutor ventured one last question, "Do you think the Vicar might have murdered her?"

"Good Lord no. She always said he would tell her off if she spoke about leaving him money. I didn't come down here very often but whenever I did, it seemed to me they adored each other."

Even when the witness had begun to give evidence, Ronnie Redpath had been undecided about whether to mention the questionable date on the hotel bill. In the end, when the time came for his cross examination, he decided to ask just one question.

"Did you stop for breakfast on your journey down that morning?"

"I did I had arranged to meet her at eleven and there was no point getting there early as Aunt Em said she would be going down to the church to sort the flowers out first.

"Thank you. No further questions"

Both the Magistrates and his fellow barrister looked rather mystified as to why this question had been asked but put it down to a young man who felt he had to justify his fee.

There being no further witnesses for the prosecution and with Mr Redpath's indication that the defence would not be calling any witnesses, the Bench retired.

Sometimes a Bench will retire for the sake of appearances and partake of a cup of tea before returning with its decision. On this occasion, there was a short but genuine consideration.

"I don't think I would convict a Vicar on the evidence we have," said one of the lady wingers adjusting her hat which had brushed against the top of the door as they retired.

"I'm inclined to agree with you," said the Chair, "but our decision is just whether or not there is a case to answer."

The third member of the Bench had busied herself pouring tea from a pot which had just been delivered. "Well, I think it's highly suspicious. You do take milk don't you Mr Parsons?"

The Chair of the Bench confirmed that he did and then asked do we agree then that we should send the defendant for trial. His lady colleagues nodded their agreement. But the trio then spent a few minutes drinking their tea and discussing interesting points from the evidence. Mr Parsons shared his opinion that it was a bit like a Dickson Carr locked door murder mystery. They then rose to return to Court led by the lady who had poured the tea and with the magistrate with the rather large hat carefully ducking through the door as she brought up the rear.

"We feel there is a case to answer and consequently you will be sent for trial at the Assize Court." This would have sufficed but whether to salve his conscience about doubting the word of a man of the cloth or to show his knowledge of the law he added, "This does not mean we think you are guilty merely that there is a case to answer."

Before he could go further, the Clerk to the Justices cut in, "Thank you Sir. I understand there is to be no bail application Mr Redpath.

"Those are my instructions"

"In that case," said the Clerk anxious to get things over with before his Chair of the Bench made some injudicious comment, "Mr O'Donnell, you will be informed of the date for your trial in due course. Can you go with the officers now."

Ronnie Redpath's journey home involved a stop to change trains, which afforded him time to do two things. Firstly, he used the phone box on the station to ring Moira McKenzie, to tell her the news that his client had been sent for trial and secondly, to drop in the post box at the station, the breakfast receipt in an envelope addressed to the Swanage Police Force CID Department.

Chapter Eighteen

Patients' Suspicions

The excellent climate of Swanage not only attracted public benefactors like George and Elizabeth Burt to establish a hospital in the area but many individuals interested in a healthy climate in which to spend their retirements while easing any ills from which they suffered. These meant there was always plenty of work to keep Nurse Mackenzie busy. Driving away from her visit to one such couple, the Rays, her mind was preoccupied. It was not the condition of her patient, whose varicose vein problem was improving, albeit slowly, but the words of her husband. As he usually did, her husband had talked almost incessantly. He explained his role on D Day, why he had missed out on playing in a Test match for England and his relationship with Winston Churchill. None of this had concerned Moira, who had heard it all before and attributed it to a medical condition the name of which she could not quite recall. It had been his returning on three occasions, to a more recent event, namely Emily Henderson's murder that stuck in her mind. No less than three times, he had mentioned an old tramp with a red beard. Could this be the person who had murdered Miss Henderson? If so, how had they managed to get into the church without being seen? Preoccupied with these thoughts, she almost went through a red light just managing to brake sharply before she did so. This seemed to shock her and she resolved to think no more about it at present. God had put her on earth to save lives as a nurse, not to kill people as a careless driver. She would share her thoughts she decided with Sergeant Brownlow, until which time she resolved to stop playing detective and concentrate on the job she was paid for.

At roughly the same time as these events were happening, just outside the village of Lyddcastle, in his office in Swanage, Mr Daltry was finishing writing up the minutes of a meeting he had just attended and, having done so, picked up some papers and went through to his Secretary's Office.

"If you would be good enough to type these up and make five copies," he requested, "and I just wonder if you would be good enough to witness my signature on this document." He placed it in front of his Secretary who compliantly signed it, as she frequently did for his clients.

"Certainly Mr Daltry. Will you be needing copies of the Minutes this afternoon?"

"No, Tomorrow will be fine. I will also sort out the distribution of them tomorrow morning."

Although it was not normally his habit to drink at lunchtime the decision of the meeting he had just attended, coupled with the document his Secretary had just signed, led him to decide a small sherry in the lounge of the Victoria Hotel might be in order and he deftly lifted his hat from the stand in the corner of the room and waved farewell to his Secretary, and with an assurance he would be back by two o'clock, he took his leave.

It was around four o'clock in the afternoon and Doctor Carrington was reclining on the sofa in his sitting room, gently running his fingers over the stockinged feet on his lap. "After a couple more years and you will be able to take the weight of these a lot more often."

"Yes," responded Miss Standish, the owner of the feet in question. "That meeting of shareholders this morning certainly seems to have cleared the way. I must say, Archibald Daltry seemed awfully keen to push it through quickly. Not like most solicitors."

"Wanted to get it done while he has executor's powers, makes life easier for him. Did you notice he got everyone to agree to his firm handling of all of the conveyance involved, that will be worth a bob or two."

Miss Standish seemed little concerned about this but did venture "Who cares? The thing is with his reputation and involvement with the church, he should be able to defuse any objections."

At this point Doctor Carrington slid gently on top of Miss Standish who, not being on duty until six the next morning, raised no objection at all and snuggled gently beneath the arms that enfolded her. "And he will be pleased to know that one of your patients old Mrs. Nelson reckons it wasn't the Vicar who murdered Miss Henderson" and, added the Doctor, "She claims she knows who did it."

"And who was that," she asked gently removing the Doctor's hand, which was slipping in to places she rather thought it shouldn't. The pain killers Mrs Nelson was on, meant she was away with the fairies half the time, but what had put the murder in her head, she wondered.

"Oh, that would be patient confidentiality," said the Doctor smiling and carefully placing his hand to its former position on Miss Standish. She smiled and this time left his hand exactly where it was.

Chapter Nineteen

Nurse Mackenzie's call to arms

That evening saw a meeting of the Bell Ringers, who had met at the insistence of Nurse Mackenzie. After they had sorted the reduced number of ringing activities brought about by the Vicar's incarceration, she explained why she had been so anxious to get them together. "Look gentlemen," she began, "I believe and I hope you do too, that the Reverend John is innocent." The term the Reverend John was well chosen, conveying both a respect for rank and friendship. "I believe we should all share whatever we know to try and secure his acquittal. There are things I want to share with you that I can only do if we are agreed on that point. Are you with me?"

By nods and vocal assents, the entire company indicated their agreement.

"In which case I suggest we start by promising to share any information or ideas we have and not to act in any way that betrays our Vicar."

Old Tom, who could not have hoped for a better reason to share his worry, immediately signalled his agreement, nodding his head and saying "Excellent idea. If we cannot believe each other how can we expect a jury to?"

Her other three companions were less enthusiastic. In fact, Daltry, after some fiddling with a ring on his finger, snorted, "I am afraid as a solicitor my first loyalty is to my clients and there is no way I could agree to such a "Boy Scout" sort of pact. I think it would probably be as well if I left you now." With this, he drained his sherry glass and swept out of the bar, gathering his hat as he did so.

Sergeant Brownlow had been staring at his feet. In fact, he was rather pleased Daltry had left as for some reason he always made him seem rather uncomfortable due to the conflicting roles that could occur in their professional life, but the need to socialise while doing a hobby in which they shared enjoyment. At length, he spoke, "As long as we are not expecting anyone to lie, that's fine by me. We shall have to tell the truth in the witness box, so we might as well share it with each other now."

"There is something I want to get off my chest. It's about that morning when Emily was murdered." It was Old Tom who spoke seeming anxious to commit himself to speaking but then being unsure of what to say. "Look," he said "I can honestly say I have answered the questions put to me honestly, but there was something else that I have half convinced myself I imagined and if I had spoken out I would at worst have seemed to implicate the Vicar, who I am damned sure, pardon my language, Moira, didn't and wouldn't ever kill an old lady and at best I'd merely muddy the waters."

"Well come on Tom. Spit it out," implored Moira rather inelegantly.

"It's like this. I have never told a lie, least ways not to the police. They asked me had I seen anyone go in to the church and I said what I had seen, honest to God I did, but no one ever asked about people coming out."

"You mean someone coming out of the church? Where from?" Interrupted Sergeant Brownlow.

"Yes, from the Vestry Door leastways I thought so." Clearly distressed he mopped his forehead and picked up his pint, before putting it down again without drinking.

"I thought I saw a bloke in a surplice come running out and disappear across the churchyard."

"You mean the Vicar," came the voice of Moira.

"No, it can't have been, he had a red beard and he was shorter than our Vicar."

"How can it have been anyone else?" asked Sergeant Brownlow, "He and Emily were the only ones in the Church."

"That's why I haven't mentioned it. I would readily swear on the bible nobody cept the Vicar went in, so how could I say someone else came out?"

"You were very specific though re height and a red beard," observed the Sergeant.

"That's why it is so difficult. If I swear to it, I'm lying about no one going in."

"Calm down Tom. We know you are an honest man. You have to accept you might have been mistaken," Moira laid a comforting hand on his shoulder.

"You don't think I am going like ga ga. People will say I am going loony and have me put away."

"Of course they won't," came the comforting tones of the Nurse, "If everyone who made an honest mistake was put way there would not be establishments big enough in Christendom to hold them. Besides, there are other possibilities. There might be another way in to the church, perhaps someone was already in the church, even before our practice." She continued less confidently, "Perhaps it was the Vicar and your mind refuses to accept it."

"Quite true Moira, but, if it was the Vicar running away, how come he was in the church when the alarm was raised?" questioned the Sergeant. His mind was teeming and he was anxious to get away so seeking to end the meeting he said "Never you fear Tom, unless we are questioned under oath, we won't say anything about this."

"Yes Tom, you can rely on us," reassured Moira. "There is one other thing I need to share with you both though. It's about a receipt that the nephew gave me." With that she explained her concerns.

This and the rest of what had happened was explained by the Nurse to Ronnie Redford in a phone call that evening. What Ronnie had to tell her was less pleasing. The QC who was in charge of the case had informed Ronnie that he was going to travel down to see the Vicar in prison to take instructions for the trial. Ronnie was still to be involved to the extent that he had been asked to review the brief, to look for weaknesses in the Crown's case. What really worried Nurse Mackenzie was what Ronnie said next.

"Weaknesses, it would be harder to look for any strengths. It's a complete travesty that he should be on trial. They wouldn't try to make a case like this stick on an old lag, but they are so anxious not to show favouritism, they are sticking an innocent Vicar in the dock. What is unbelievable is that old Barratt Is going to try to get the Vicar to plead guilty to manslaughter, saying it was an accident, as that would explain away the forensic evidence."

"That's utter tosh," exclaimed Moira, "even that Inspector Crawford explained there could be innocent explanations to all of it."

"I know, but it means they will be able to call a couple of expert witnesses, people at old Barratt's Club. It will be jobs for the boys. There is not a lot I can say to cheer you up but, I will go through the brief again but there is not much I expect to find that will help."

"Can you do something for me? Get me called as a witness for the defence," pleaded Moira down the phone.

"On what grounds? Did you ever treat Miss Henderson?"

"Yes."

"In that case, it should not be a problem. It could help a case that it was an accident, frail elderly lady having medical treatment. It would mean challenging the pathologist's evidence though old Barratt would like that I expect he has a specialist who will agree to say anything if the money is right."

When the Bell Ringers, minus their solicitor member who had pleaded a previous engagement, gathered the following evening, Sergeant Brownlow had something to show them. "It arrived in the post this morning." he explained. I am not sure it helps at all in our efforts on behalf of the Vicar but given our agreement I think I ought to share it. It's a letter from my old colleague I met when I went up to Oxford with Moira. I will read it to you.

Dear George,

It was good to meet up and talk over old times. I have done as you asked and seen what I could find out about the chap you enquired about. I must say it was quite like old times going out and sort of interviewing people. Strange people seem more relaxed when the chap they talk to does not have a uniform on, like I did before I hung up my truncheon.

I suspect young Henderson is like many students - thought rather more highly of by his fellow students than his Dons. The Dons describe him as rather spasmodic in his attitude to his studies. He is a poor attendee at lectures but gets his essays in on time, although they often appear rushed and of a low standard. He might get a third, which I am told is the mark of a gentleman, if the examiners are feeling generous which, given his involvement in college activities they probably will. A Don who was on the Committee of the OUDS did speak rather better of him. Thought he was a very promising actor who, he thought, deserved better parts than he usually got. I asked him why he thought this was and he looked thoughtful for a couple of moments before volunteering a couple of reasons. The first was that he was not good at remembering his lines, the second that he upset the Costume People by losing things.

The student who was in the room next door in college confirmed much of the above explaining how he was likely to be wearing half his costume in the pub afterwards, have too much to drink and leave bits behind. He was also able to help with your particular interest in what happened on the morning of your murder. He recalls him coming in to his room early the next morning. He told him he was going down to see his Aunt. It was about six o'clock and he said he could not face her on an empty stomach so wanted to try to make time for a decent breakfast on the way. He offered him a cup of coffee but said he could not stop, and pointed to the clock over there. It was a brown mahogany one on the mantelpiece. The only other thing that might be of relevance is that he was wearing a long overcoat which his friend said he often did, as he liked to drive with the open top of his car down.

"I will leave it there because the rest is just about meeting up again and how he spends his time in retirement." The Sergeant waited for any comments from his three companions but none spoke.

"One other thing you might like to think about. It may bear out what Tom was talking about yesterday. When I was reading through the statement the Vicar made, he said that he had put his coat in the main church because his surplice was on the only coat hook in the vestry. I checked with Inspector Crawford, as I felt sure he would have noted whether it was or not. He admitted he had not, explaining nobody had mentioned someone leaving the church wearing a surplice but anyway, by the time he got involved, any items hung or not hung on the vestry door could have been replaced or removed."

Chapter Twenty

The Trial

The trial of the Reverend John O'Donnell was due to open on the second Tuesday in June. That morning saw an anxious Redpath, who had travelled down from London the previous night anxiously awaiting the arrival of his learned leader, Bartholomew Barratt QC, who he had been informed hoped to join him that morning but if he did not, to ask for an adjournment. The entry of the Judge with no sign of Mr Barratt made him realise this was the course of action he would have to take and he rose to ask for an adjournment. Despite speaking as apologetically and deferentially as he could he received a rather frosty reception from the Judge.

"May I ask why our learned friend, Mr Barrett, has not favoured us with his presence?"

"I am afraid he is involved in a case in the High Court, which has overrun. I believe the case he was involved in was scheduled to finish last week but with disruption caused by the cancellation of sittings for the coronation it has overrun and needed extra days."

"No doubt along with healthy refresher fees for the extra days of the case. Well, Mr Redpath, it will not do. A respected member of the community is in custody. Are you aware Mr Redpath that her gracious Majesty is the Head of the Church of which your client is a member?"

"Indeed, I am Sir."

I am sure her gracious Majesty would not wish her Coronation to be responsible for lengthening the period of incarceration of a Minister of her church. I am loathed to extend the period of prisoners awaiting trial just so lawyers can earn extra fees. Are you not a qualified barrister?"

"Yes, your Honour. I suppose I am"

"And you have studied the papers relating to the case?"

"Very carefully your Honour", answered Redpath truthfully.

"Then you may well have an advantage over Mr Barratt whose excellent legal brain has no doubt been focused elsewhere. Mr O'Donnell, have you any observations on why you should not be represented by Mr. Redpath before this Court?"

"With respect your Honour, God is the only Judge whose findings concern me so for me representation in this Court is immaterial."

"In which case, while I have to consider that you are properly represented to ensure a fair trial, the fact that you have a fully qualified young barrister to represent you seems to make that possible. I see no reason to delay this trial. Mr Bradshaw you may open your case."

At this, the ample figure of E C Bradshaw QC rose. A black and brown striped waistcoat just managed to contain his stomach beneath a dark suit and robes . He spoke saying, "I am much obliged your honour."

Six words for the Judge were sufficient. It was the jury that would decide on a verdict, so Mr Bradshaw turned to them and it was to them fellow members, of what he termed the sane and sensible representatives of their country, that he addressed his opening remarks.

"I have a very simple task this morning, to lay before you the facts. I begin with the caution that it is not up to my learned friend, Mr. Redpath to prove his client's innocence but for me to prove, beyond all reasonable doubt, his guilt. To do this I will call a number of witnesses, but first, let me set out the circumstances in which this poor old lady, Miss Henderson, was cruelly murdered."

Bradshaw's opening address was comparatively short, focusing on two main points. These being that an expert medical professional had conducted a post mortem which showed death was incontrovertibly caused by suffocation, and that the only person in the church at the relevant time was the defendant.

The remainder of the morning of the trial saw two witnesses take the stand after the introduction of the Prosecuting barrister. The first took no more than ten minutes. A small, bespectacled man with a toothbrush moustache who testified that he had made the diagram of the church, copies of which had been distributed to the jury and trial participants.

He was followed by Mrs Hinton. There had been some discussion between the prosecuting team as to whether they should put her on the stand before or after the pathologist, who had discovered that Miss Henderson's demise had not been due to natural causes. In the same way that AJ Bryant believed that history was a chronological story and should be presented as such Bradshaw believed you should deal with the case so that it unfolded to the jury as it happened. It was important he felt that you did not leave witnesses subject to a cross examination of a hindsight they had not possessed but with which a jury possessing the same might think them unreliable.

No mention was made of lambs being swung over heads, so Mrs Hinton appeared a persuasive witness. It was explained how, at the instigation of her husband, she had made a written record of events. Her story was given sadly, but without unnecessary elaboration. She told of her arrival at the Church, the door being open, Old Tom seeing her and her shock at seeing Miss Henderson leaning over the font.

Only one piece of the examination gave Redpath cause for concern and this was due to Bradshaw's question, "When you first saw Miss Henderson lying unconscious did you think she was dead?"

"Good Lord no. Whenever I had seen her Miss Henderson seemed full of life. I could imagine her having a fainting fit but not dying."

"Who first suggested that Miss Henderson was dead?" queried the prosecuting Counsel.

"Why the Vicar."

Only three words, but was it a pessimistic outlook that had the man charged with defending the aforesaid Vicar to think of a jury man thinking "well if he killed her, he would know she was wouldn't he." It would be a statement not a question.

At this point, a master of his craft, Bradshaw a master of his craft pronounced "No further questions," and with a flourish of his gown resumed his seat.

When he had read the brief, Redpath had realised a dilemma. Did he leave 'the whited sepulchre' that was the reputation of Miss Henderson unstained or raise the point that she could be seen as a bossy, self-opinionated and self-righteous person who could very easily get on your nerves. He decided on balance to leave 'the whited sepulchre' alone. People did not kill one another for causing them annoyance and if they did the Vicar would have a better reason than many for removing a Church Warden, whose relationship with him was not an entirely straight forward one in some people's eyes. Hence, he rose and looking Mrs Hinton in the eye and said "I have only one question. Do you think Mr. O'Donnell killed this lady?"

"What our Vicar, kill someone, no it's not in his nature."

Glancing at the prosecutor as if to say fifteen all, Redpath resumed his seat.

After lunch Archibald Daltry, Solicitor and bell ringer, was called to the witness box. Identifying who he was and what he was, took rather longer than it might have done had he not insisted on elaborating every answer. The jury needed to know he was a solicitor but did they really need to know he was the third generation of his family to be a member of the firm with dates and service of his predecessors? That he had been responsible for Miss Henderson's will was obvious but needed stating, but did he need to add the fact that she always asked for him by name on account of his godly reputation for honest, Christian virtue, or that the late lamented sister, Miss Henderson the Elder, had always felt and done the same. Eventually, the prosecutor was able to get Mr Daltry to confirm that Mr O'Connell stood to benefit from Miss Henderson's will and might have not done so had Miss Henderson been alive and able to attend her meeting with him on the Tuesday following her death.

"So," concluded Mr Barratt, "Mr O'Connell had a very clear motive to murder Miss Henderson. Is that not true?"

"I am afraid so."

"Thank you, No further questions."

"In which case," intoned the judge, "I believe you may cross examine Mr Redpath." The words carried the tone of one who believed there would have to be a cross examination but the hope that it would be short enough to enable him to adjourn for a brief comfort break, to enable him less to relieve his bladder as to see if his attendant had been able to obtain a paper with the latest cricket scores.

Emboldened by his brief but effective cross examination of Mrs Hinton, Redpath, seeing himself as a later day Marshall Hall and, beginning to worry as much about the impression his questions would have on Nurse Mackenzie as the jury, rose and clutched his lapels in a very fair imitation of the prosecutor and began his short cross examination.

"You have told us how Miss Henderson thought sufficiently highly of Mr O'Donnell as to reward him in her will?"

Mr Daltry seemed a little less self-assured when he realised he was to be cross examined but, faced with this opening question, he relaxed. "That is so."

"But did not anyone else also receive similar generosity from Miss Henderson?"

"They did."

At this point Redpath's inexperienced betrayed him in to asking one question too many.

"So might they not equally have wanted to kill Miss Henderson before she met you."

"Yes", responded the solicitor, "but they were nowhere near the church, so they could not have killed her."

Realising his error, Redpath subsided to his seat. In the gallery, Nurse Mackenzie glowered at her fellow bell ringer and, with her nurse's knowledge of the sensitivity of a males' testicles, imagined seven types of torment she would have liked to inflict on his.

The following witness, Old Tom, was less anti-Vicar, but his evidence was no more helpful to the Defence. He was adamant that there was no one in the church when he left it.

"So only someone, such as the Vicar, who had a key, could have been in the Church." suggested Bradshaw.

Old Tom was probably closer to facing his maker and as such weighed his words carefully. "That's true, but he would no way kill Miss Henderson cepting it was for her own good."

The final witness of the day was Doctor Carrington. The prosecution team did not think he would have much, if anything, to add to the case against Mr O'Connell, but he felt it wise to have an experienced GP neutralised by giving evidence for the prosecution rather than giving evidence for the Defence. He realised many jurors would be more impressed by the evidence of a common or garden GP than a specialist with an alphabet of letters after his name. Such a respected GP, having thought Miss Henderson had died of natural causes, might be enough to create a doubt and result in an acquittal, unless they themselves admitted they were in error.

Having taken Dr Carrington through how and by whom he had been called to the church, the prosecutor came to the key part of his examination. "Can I ask what you originally thought had been the cause of Miss Henderson's death?"

"Natural causes," began the Doctor confidently, "To be more specific, I thought she had had a heart attack."

"You now agree that this was a mistake?"

"That is a little blunt. I would prefer to call it an incorrect diagnosis."

"Indeed, a diagnosis which, without the full facts and equipment the best of Doctors might make."

Seeing he was not to be portrayed as a doddering incompetent, Dr Carrington opened up. "As you say I did not have the equipment that my illustrious colleague had and of course, my mind set was on helping an old lady who I had been told was ill. To be confronted with a dead body was quite a shock."

Redpath had realised that, if the impossibility of a respected Vicar to commit a crime was part of his case, that he would be ill advised to challenge the evidence of the much respected local Doctor. He did however venture on a line of questioning which, he felt, he could turn to advantage in his summing up, whatever the Doctor's evidence.

"You gave evidence that as far as you were aware Miss Henderson had no enemies?"

"That is correct."

"Is it not true though that Miss Henderson had been very outspoken against the Nursing Home, where her sister had died."

"People may have said this, but Miss Henderson had said nothing about the matter to myself directly. So, I think I am correct in saying, that under the laws of evidence, it would be wrong for me to say more."

The prosecutor was rising when Redpath said "You are perfectly correct and I certainly would not question you further on the issue, but you were, I believe, the Doctor of Miss Henderson's sister?"

"Yes," replied Carrington, wondering where this was going.

"And you could confirm as such that Miss Henderson's sister, resident at the Woodside Lodge Nursing Home at the time of her death, died from entirely natural causes, as one would expect from a lady in her nineties?"

"Yes, quite so."

"And who, can I ask, certified Miss Henderson Senior's death as being natural causes?"

"Why, I did."

"No further questions," said Redpath resuming his seat, but as he did so, looking at the jurors as much as to say 'well what a surprise.'

Bradshaw had not become a QC without the ability to think on his feet.

"Emily Henderson, or perhaps we should term her Miss Henderson Junior, seems to have thought she was, dare we say, "hastened in her passing, by the Nursing Home. Would that have been to the Nursing Homes advantage?"

"Quite the reverse. The longer she lived the more money it would make from her fees."

This would have sufficed, but Dr Carrington had more to add. "I can understand Miss Henderson's behaviour though. It was grief. It is difficult to accept that the due course of nature will take from us, even the best of us, those we love. God-fearing woman that she was, I do not believe Emily would have accepted this. She would seek to rationalise this and I fear this led her to look for someone to blame."

Neither barrister seemed to have anything to add and the Judge brought the day's proceedings to a close with thanks to the Doctor and reminding everyone that the Court would resume at ten the next morning.

In the foyer, Dr Carrington was met by Miss Standish, who linked arms with him and ushered him away. If he had come to Court fearing he was to be pilloried as an incompetent Doctor, he was now, in his own eyes, being seen as an accomplice to not just one murder, but two murders.

Redpath had wasted little time on deciding whether or not to put his client in the witness box. It was, he thought, one of those situations where a reputation for honesty could act against a defendant. If they were expected to be an honest person, was not a failure to answer questions a signal to a jury that they had something to hide. Besides, at the end of the day, it was his client's decision and O'Donnell had made it very clear he wanted the opportunity to give evidence. His barrister had explained the difficulty in proving a negative and that all he had to do was to create a reasonable doubt in the minds of the jury. Faced with a plaintiff "But I am innocent, and I want to prove it," explained that was what a not guilty verdict showed, and the best way to achieve it was to accept the way that he would examine him in the witness box.

Redpath's examination in chief, which began the next day of the trial, lasted a little less than five minutes. Having ascertained his name and that his occupation was Vicar of St Anselm's, Redpath turned to his relationship with Miss Henderson, which O'Donnell answered that she was a highly valued Church Warden and had been known to him in that capacity during the whole of his ministry at St Anselm's.

Redpath concluded with the question "Did you murder Miss Henderson?"

"No, I most certainly did not," came the clear and confident reply.

Thanking him, Redpath resumed his seat.

Shocked by the brevity of the examination, Bradshaw covered his surprise and bought himself a little time by shuffling his papers that lay in front of him. He had planned the points he intended to raise with the defendant, but had not been expected to embark on them so soon.

"In the statement you made to the police, you describe how you were preparing your sermon in the Vestry, which serves as your office, and first saw Miss Henderson on account of needing to check a quotation in the Bible on the Lectern. Was there no bible in the Vestry?"

"Yes, but the print was too small to read without my glasses."

"But you did have your glasses, didn't you?"

"Yes, but I did not realise it. They had slipped through the lining of my pocket."

"Slipped through the lining of my pocket," repeated the prosecutor in a somewhat sarcastic fashion, casting a sly glance at the jury to see if he could detect any reactions.

"Either way you went in to the main body of the church and saw Miss Henderson in your words "looking in to the font."

"That is correct."

"Did you speak to her?"

"No."

"Is it true to say you ignored her and went back in to the Vestry?"

"Unfortunately, that is correct."

"Did it not occur to you to ask this," Bradshaw looked at his notes and read, 'Much valued Church Warden', if she was alright or what she was doing?"

"To my eternal shame I did not."

"What did you think she was doing?"

"I don't know, perhaps she was looking at the font being dirty, that is half the reason for not speaking to her. I was afraid I'd be given a lecture. She was always very fussy about the appearance of the church, 'Cleanliness is next to Godliness' she would always remind me."

"An annoying lady, was she?"

"At times."

"I put it to you that this was one of those times. She complained about something once too often and you lost your temper. Perhaps you did not mean to kill her, just give her a good shaking, until you realised what you were doing or had done."

"I never touched her."

"But in your statement to the police you say 'you checked to see if she was alive and you put a coat over her."

"Yes, but that was later, I had been nowhere near her until I heard Mrs Hinton screaming."

"You said at one point you had no glasses and then you found them?"

"Well, I did."

"You have answers for everything, don't you, but can we believe them? No further questions".

The Vicar looked about to say something but before he could, his barrister, Mr Redpath indicated he had no re-examination questions and that Mr O'Donnell should return to the dock.

Redpath then turned to the Judge and said, "With your permission, can I have two items entered as exhibits, before my next witness gives her evidence?"

After a minute or two of confusion as the prosecuting barrister looked at the prosecuting solicitor, who fumbled through a large case beneath his seat before producing the two items that Mr Redpath had indicated. These were the Diary found at Miss Henderson's house and the breakfast bill. The Judge directed that these were to be referred to as Exhibits D and E respectively, and indicated that Mr Redpath could call his witness.

Nurse Mackenzie appeared wearing her nurse's uniform which she had agreed would make a good impression. Having established who she was, and that she was the District Nurse and a bell ringer, Redpath explained she was part character witness, but also to explain the two exhibits.

This prompted the prosecutor to interject, "I am sure we shall listen to what Nurse Mackenzie has to say in relation to the defendant's character, but I can scarcely see what relevance these two documents have to the case."

The Judge, clearly rather smitten by the appearance of a comely nurse in her starched uniform, smiled. "It may be relevant, or it may not. I will certainly advise the jury accordingly. Until I have heard what light, if any, these exhibits cast on the case, I can hardly judge. Pray proceed Mr Redpath."

Having got his witness to explain how she had come to know the Vicar and to vouch for him as a 'Pillar of the local community' and a kindly man who exhibited all the qualities one would expect from a minister of the cloth, he turned to the exhibits.

"I believe that the diary was found by you and handed to the police?"

"That's correct."

"What did you think it contained that might be of interest to them in regard to this case?"

"One of the things, I believe it's called circumstantial evidence, that has brought the Reverend O'Donnell into the dock, is that

Miss Henderson was going to change her will." The diary shows that this was something she had told her nephew about and that she might be going to revise her will in a way that was detrimental to him."

"So do you think that Miss Henderson was murdered by her nephew?"

This had Bradshaw on his feet. "Your honour, is that a proper question?"

Before his honour could respond, Nurse Mackenzie had given the Jury her answer, "If I say that I do not, and that on the contrary, he is a charming young man who gave me a delightful tour of Oxford's dreaming spires, I can no more see him as a murderer than I can the Vicar. It is just that it is very easy to read more in to true facts than is actually justified."

The Judge beamed, knowing he no longer needed to slap down a member of the nursing profession, but could still avoid slapping down the prosecuting barrister for his interjection. "Your objection was well justified, but given Miss Mackenzie's answer it can hardly be seen as something I need task the jury to ignore. Mr, um, whatever this nephew's name is, is not on trial and any aspirations on him would be uncalled for. Miss Mackenzie has made none. Indeed, she seems to have given him a character reference. Pray continue Mr Redpath, but remember, it is only the guilt or innocence of Mr O'Donnell that is a matter for this Court today."

"I will indeed your honour. I had intended to conclude at this point anyway and your honour has convinced me that is indeed the correct course."

"You have entered a breakfast receipt in evidence, have you no wish to ask this witness questions about it?" asked the judge.

"No, your honour. It is thanks to Miss Mackenzie that it has been brought to light but her opinion of it is not something which should need to concern this Court. I hope, however, that your honour will permit me to refer to it in my summing up."

"That is entirely a matter for you. If you feel it in anyway speaks to the innocence of your client you will undoubtedly do so. In case of that eventuality, Mr Usher, will you please show the witness exhibit E."

This was done and the witness duly confirmed that this was the receipt and how it came into her possession. Pausing the judge turned to the prosecution side.

"Before I release the witness have you any questions about the receipt or any other matter?"

The prosecutor having given a negative response, the Judge dismissed the witness with thanks.

With Redpath having indicated that he had no further witnesses, the summing up by both barristers followed. Neither raised anything that had not already been mentioned but both put a slant on it so that it slanted to the guilt or innocence of the defendant, depending on the role they had to play. Redpath made two points in regard to the breakfast receipt prefacing them placed on them. Firstly, he commented on how easy it was to forget about something in a jacket pocket. If Mr Henderson had mislaid a receipt which could prove his innocence how much easier was it for his client, Mr O'Donnell to mislay his glasses. Secondly, he drew attention to the date. "Had it been issued on the 17th or the 11th?" asked Redpath." It was clearly issued on the 17th as Mr Henderson confirms it as does the waitress who issued it who does not work on Saturdays. Why would he lie to create an alibi he does not need as he is not accused yet it clearly does not look right. Is that not the same though as many things about my client's actions in the church on that Friday morning. They may not look right but does that make him a murderer?" He concluded with an oration which would have been worthy of Sir Edward Marshall Hall. "Lady and gentlemen of the jury,* there stands before you an innocent man, put where he is by an awful sequence of mishaps and misjudgements. Which of us has not mislaid their glasses, if we wear them, or has not averted our eyes and passed by on the other side, due to having things to do we considered more important, yet it is these things that have brought the Reverend O'Donnell before you today. Indeed, more than this, it is his own obstinate honesty that has put him where he is. He had only to say 'I might have left the door off the latch' and no power on earth would have put him where he is. His own honesty puts his life in jeopardy. He still has one thing to save him, the presumption of innocence, a silver thread that runs through the English system of justice of which we are rightly so proud. If it is a presumption that is extended to the lowest scoundrel, should it no more be extended to an upright and virtuous man like the one who stands before you today. Be true to the oath you have taken and acquit my client."

At this point the Judge called a short adjournment. On this occasion it was nothing to do with catching up with the latest cricket scores although the first thing he intended to do when the Court rose was to check the evening paper stop press to find how Somerset were getting on against Kent at the Bath Festival. He needed time to give himself a chance to get his notes in order for his summing up and to afford the jury to enjoy a cup of tea and a stretch of legs before checking through the notes of his summing up.. Around fifteen minutes later all parties were summoned to return to Court and the familiar cry of "All rise" signalled the return of his honour, bringing a splash of red to the Bench.

Chapter Twenty One

A Summation and a verdict

Turning to face the jury the judge noted how the single lady magistrate was wedged in at the end of the back row. She had sat there throughout the trial and he guessed it was the curtesy of ladies first that meant she had to sit cheek by jowl next to only one man rather than being squeezed between two. "Members of the jury", he began "So far, your role has been a very passive one. Now, you will be required to play an active, indeed may I say, critical role in deciding on the guilt or innocence of the accused. My job is to summarise the evidence. In terms of the law, you must follow what I say but, in matters of fact, it is your view and your view that matters and, what I say in regard to that, you must feel free to disregard if your view differs. I will begin, more or less, where Mr Redpath, very eloquently I may say, finished. You only convict if you are certain that the defendant is guilty. I use the term defendant advisedly for not for nothing is the figure of justice depicted as being blindfolded. For justice to be done all men should be treated equally and, it matters not whether the accused is the Archbishop of Canterbury or the most inveterate burglar in the country, they should be accorded this same right."

"The second point I must make is in regard to what should be relevant to your considerations. In that regard I must say it is what you have heard in Court and not what you have heard or read outside of these Court walls. Perhaps this is a point where I should refer to something which has troubled me throughout this case. I may be a Judge but I am also human and having heard the evidence I must say that I rather hope that none of you, like my wife, are readers of Agatha Christie or others of her ilk. We are not dealing here with a fictional "locked room mystery" but a real-life issue of life and death and real people. On the evidence you have heard in this Court it is not disputed that Miss Henderson was unlawfully killed. On the evidence you have heard only one person was in the Church at the time of her death, which, the Prosecution claim, and the Defence do not deny was due to suffocation. This the Prosecution claim is sufficient to convict the defendant for although the evidence is circumstantial - it is compelling. At this point I should explain to you what we mean by circumstantial evidence. To give an example: if a man is on the same bus as a murder victim that would be circumstantial evidence. If they were the only other person on the bus while that might make the evidence more compelling it would still be circumstantial although you might think it more compelling. Turning from circumstantial evidence to forensic evidence a blood stain matching that of the victim on a defendant or a finger print of the accused on a knife found in the body of a victim would be forensic evidence. It is one of the complicating matters of this case that what might seem forensic evidence against the accused is in fact circumstantial. To his eternal credit, this has been mentioned to us by Inspector Crawford. The fact that fibres from a pew cushion were found both on the clothes of the Vicar and on the face of the victim could have perfectly innocent explanations and do not prove that the Vicar used it to suffocate Miss Henderson. So, in a way, even forensic evidence can quite easily become merely circumstantial. The facts of the case have been laid before you and upon those facts what we can believe is a matter for you. However, in matters of law, you must accept my words. The law states that to be guilty of murder one must have "malice aforethought," in everyday language to have planned to do it. I do not believe anything has been given in evidence to hold the Vicar guilty of planning to murder Miss Henderson. Did he know Miss Henderson would be present in church? No. In fact it was quite contrary in that Miss Henderson had varied her normal routine and was in church much earlier than was her normal habit. We have no evidence the Defendant knew this even less that Miss Henderson was to visit her solicitor with a view to amending her will. It would be my view, and one you must accept, as no evidence to the contrary has been laid before you, that Mr O'Donnell is not guilty of murder."

In the gallery, a warm glow came over Nurse Mackenzie while on the counsel's Bench a deep feeling of relief was felt by Mr Redpath. Both feelings were short lived as the Judge continued.

"You have heard considerable and, dare I say, compelling evidence that in fact the only person who could have brought a premature end to Miss Henderson's life was the defendant as he was the only person present and that her premature demise was the work of a human agency, not natural causes. It does seem almost irreconcilable that a seemingly honest man, even to his own detriment saying he was sure the Vestry Door was locked, could have knowingly done it. Perhaps he had a fit of amnesia. We have heard how he struck his head, perhaps that had affected him. Perhaps his mind is so horrified by what he has done that it has genuinely blanked it out in the same way that people involved in car crashes have no recollection of the events. I think that this is the point where I should put the matter in your hands under English law, while Mr O'Donnell is not guilty of murder he would be guilty of manslaughter. Whether you feel the weight of the mass of circumstantial evidence enables you to be sure he is guilty is a matter for you. I will now invite you to retire to consider you verdict."

Chapter Twenty Two

Archibald Daltry lends a hand

The first gathering of the Bell Ringers following the announcement of the verdict that, while not guilty of murder, their Vicar had been found guilty of manslaughter was a sombre affair. More than one of them was thinking of calling it a day. For Sergeant Brownlow, it was a feeling that the many friends of the Vicar would look at him and view him with suspicion as part of the organization which appeared to have robbed them of their Vicar. For Nurse Mackenzie there were two reasons. One was the thought that every time she pulled the bell rope her mind would be thinking of a Vicar imprisoned and disgraced and dwelling on whether she could have done any more to prevent it. On a more positive front for the first time since she had a date with one young man and was enjoying a regular exchange of letters with another. If bell- ringing clashed with such activities, she had little doubt which would go. Perhaps, sensing the atmosphere, Major Calley spoke before they had time to voice their thoughts. "It's pretty bleak at the moment I know. The church is struggling to get a replacement to take services but fortunately we are not booked to do any weddings at the moment so, we should not do anything hasty."

"I think you make a good point, Major, but I am not sure the parishioners would want me here, now the Vicar has been found guilty," sighed Brownlow.

Feeling the need to take control before further talk of leaving the group followed, the Major seized on the first point by referring to the last.

"He may have been found guilty, but the legal process has not been completed yet."

"Exactly," chimed in Old Tom, "You never can tell what the future holds. There's a fair few spring chickens as is buried in the graveyard that I never expected to outlive. An appeal could set him free."

"If he appeals," said Nurse Mackenzie, sniffing the whisky she had surprised her colleagues by ordering instead of her usual tipple.

"Well, why wouldn't he?" objected the Major.

Her first instinct was to carry on regardless, but any flutter of conscience about breaching the confidence of her correspondent was removed when she thought any second-year law student could tell them what she was about to impart.

"Firstly, he has got to have grounds," she said "and the problem is that if he appeals that the Judge should not have given the jury the option of manslaughter, it could merely result in the matter being sent for retrial. If he is found guilty then it could be he would face a meeting with the hangman God help us." This thought seemed so to distress her that she swigged back her whisky and signalled to the barman to get another round in.

"Can't they just argue that the Judge said it was manslaughter or nothing and just argue that the jury got it wrong?"

The question may have been addressed to Nurse Mackenzie, but it was Archibald Daltry, the solicitor, who incredibly had accepted the offer of a second sherry, who answered.

"I am afraid not, unless you can argue the jury's verdict was perverse, which in my mind it clearly was not."

"Says you," raged old Tom. His feeling that the Vicar and Church Warden had always been at odds seemingly justified.

"Steady down, Tom," broke in George Brownlow, "he's only telling the truth. Besides, the Vicar did not really help himself. Have any of you read what it said in the paper that he refused the offer of bail which the judge said he would grant if he was considering an appeal. The Judge indicated he was willing to listen to an application for bail and the young chap representing him got up only for Mr O'Donnell to wave him to sit down and ask to be taken back to the cells."

"And the other thing you gentlemen may or may not know is that the accused has to give his consent to an appeal and my understanding is he has refused," It was Nurse Mackenzie, who sensibly had not begun to drink her second whisky but none the less, spoke from the heart.

"Can't somebody persuade him to appeal?" asked the Major.

"My understanding," said Nurse Mackenzie, whose time spent with a young barrister had got her in the habit of speaking in a circumspect fashion, "is that he is refusing to see any visitors."

For a moment, which seemed a lot longer, there was silence before the solicitor broke in. "Look I know you don't think a lot of me. As a solicitor and a Rotary Club Treasurer, I am used to that, but I hope you will accept that I am an honest man."

"True, but look where honesty has put the Vicar," sneered Old Tom. "if tis truth that all you lawyers and Rotarians care about then you can stick it where a monkey sticks his nuts.!"

"Well, I do care about honesty," said Daltry, "and there is something I am willing to do."

Old Tom had got up and was about to depart when Brownlow pushed him down "Steady down Tom, let's hear the gentleman out."

"Thank you, Sergeant," said Daltry, using a colleague's official title as he tended to do when he was feeling unappreciated by the group. "I will try to arrange to visit Mr O'Donnell. And see if I can persuade him to appeal"

"I am sure that would be helpful," said Brownlow but I have heard he is refusing to see any visitors."

"I am sure," said the solicitor "you are right, but no one has asked to see him to address matters concerning the Church. He may have stopped wanting to help himself but, although I may not think that highly of him, I will give him credit that he would never do anything to harm or neglect the parish. If I make it clear that I need get certain elements clarified for the services and bookings in St Anselm's, I am sure he will see me."

Even old Tom had to agree it could do no harm and the others were hopeful it might do some good and it put the group in a better humour. They agreed to meet again for their normal get together the following week and to see if they could recruit any new members. New blood was always being looked for and, with resignations in the mind of one or two members, it seemed even more important.

Nurse Mackenzie was just fastening the last suspenders clip on her stocking when the phone rang. Cursing inwardly and hoping it was not a patient who she would feel morally obliged to visit, even if off duty, she was doubly delighted when the voice of Redpath came on the line. The news he imparted improved Moira's spirits even more. Having heard that the Vicar had agreed to appeal she hardly took in the rest, other than certain phrases "your solicitor chap did it", "direction to the jury." He agreed that he would write and give her the full story but he wanted to let her know, as she had been so helpful and such a boost to his morale. She thanked him and, before she knew it, the phone call was over.

Three hours later the young man, who she had been out for a meal with returned her home. She had pecked him gently on the cheek and watched him drive off with a cheerful wave to her before his car pulled swiftly away.

When she wrapped her hands around her coffee, she half wished she had invited him in but reflected it might have seemed rather forward and might she have been seen as being "fast", that greatest of all crimes in her mother's eyes. What a lovely evening she had had. Her escort had been everything a gentleman should be attentive, polite and best of all funny. He had asked about her family and she had asked about what life was like at college. Each had seemed more interested in the other and the time had passed so quickly.

She was left with one question burning in her mind. He had been confident enough to talk about a couple of former girl friends and how she was "much more alive and real, not like a Burne-Jones painting." She wondered what a girl in a Burne Jones picture looked like and how she might discreetly find out. As she unclipped her stockings, she mused how rarely she had been out with a man and how much fun it had been. Happily, she was going to see him again and smiled to herself about how readily he had agreed to come to a bell ringing session, if she went for a date with him.

Redpath was as good as his word and a couple of days later a neatly typed letter arrived i.n the post.

Dear Nurse Mackenzie,

As promised, I am just writing to let you know the details behind Mr O'Donnell agreeing to let us lodge an appeal. It is very much due to your solicitor friend. Mr. O'Donnell had refused to see us, his legal representatives, but, apparently, he asked to see him on the grounds that provisions needed to be made for the church in his absence and they needed information which only he could supply. It was from him I got the story, which I have no reason not to believe, that when he commiserated with Mr O'Donnell on his situation, he seized on your Vicar's reply that it was God's Will by saying that he did not think it was and that O'Donnell's refusal to appeal was just the act of a stubborn, self-righteous man who thought more of himself than the Church.

At first, this insult had enraged the Vicar, until he went on to say that to think God's Will was shown by a jury verdict half way through the legal process was like saying that you could understand God's Will having only read the Old Testament, and not the New. Although, at first this seemed to amuse the Vicar, after a short reflection, he said I had made a very good point, and asked whether I I realised a retrial could mean he could end up being found guilty of murder. This is all word of mouth from Daltry and he may have dressed it up a bit to make him sound good. Reading between the lines it seems he and your Vicar were not on the best of terms. He seemed to imply that if he was innocent, it should not worry the Vicar and having told the Vicar that if he was appealing, most of the information he needed could wait. He asked a couple of questions about where he could find church Rotas and left him to it.

The next thing I learned was that I was being taken off the case. I think this would have happened anyway, but I had suggested that they could appeal on the ground that that the Judge had failed to indicate that the Vicar was a man of previous good character, but it turns out he had a fine for a Public Order Offence, back before the War. Apparently, he got involved with a scuffle with some Blackshirts. All the others he was with accepted bind overs but he refused saying he had done nothing wrong and got a fine. I have to say sometimes he seems to be is his own worst enemy. Anyway, I won't bore you with legal ifs and buts suffice to say my firm's more experienced men are taking it over. While in some ways that comes as a relief, in others, I am disappointed as I won't be getting down to Dorset and seeing you. This being the case I can only say I would love it if you had time to come up to London for a day or two. I would love to show you the sites but, I expect with your job and everything, you won't want to, so all I can say is it really has been lovely having spent some time with you and wish you all the best in case we do not meet again.

It was signed Ronnie Redpath.

Oh no, Moira thought, carefully folding the letter and putting it in a drawer, you will see me again. That is if I can possibly arrange it. She had used up much off her holiday allowance to see the Court case, but thought a couple more days can be found somewhere to visit London in the not too distant future. I wonder if they have an Art Gallery with some Burne-Jones pictures. I would love to know what I don't look like.

Chapter Twenty Three

The Appeal

O nce an appeal had been decided on, the Appeal process moved remarkably quickly. Given that in murder cases it was often a requirement to get a hanging over and done with, for three Appeal Court Judges to be thrown together for half a day was not an unusual process. Within a fortnight the Appeal Court met to consider the Appeal in the case of Regina v O'Donnell.

The Court hearing itself was over in under an hour. Lord Chief Justice Goddard, who was Chairing the Appeal, was in a particularly irascible mood. "Why are we wasting time on how an unarmed Vicar killed his Church Warden? The streets are awash with armed young villains. Sometimes I wonder what the police are thinking about." Having heard from Bartholomew Barratt QC that the Appeal was on the misdirection of the jury by putting a charge of manslaughter which had not been in the original indictment and not allowing all possible options to be considered the judge's comments had led the jury to believe he thought it was a case of manslaughter and that this had been over influential in their deliberations. The Crown had no comment to make so once Bartholomew Barrett had made his submissions, their Lordships retired saying that they would give their verdict in three days later. While their Lordships agreed that the Judge should have left the decision as to murder to the jury, one of them voiced a worry.

"Would you not agree Raynor, that we should make sure that we do not give an indication that we trust judges more than juries?"

"As a generalization, that is something I would agree with," replied the Lord Chief Justice. "Too soft by half some of them, fall for any sob story."

"Well, look at those two war time cases," said his Brother Judge. There was that one where they overturned Judge Singleton on the grounds that he had over emphasised the defendant not giving an explanation for his actions three times. When the jury listened to him, and they found the rascal guilty, our predecessors overturned the verdict and turned him loose."

"Yes, I remember that Inskip, my predecessor made the decision. There were several grounds of appeal, and all of them bar that one was overturned. Can't understand it the evidence was overwhelming anyway."

"I know they found against the appeal on four points out of five, yet they never even ordered a retrial." commented the third judge.

"Yet, when a judge tells a jury they can't find a case of manslaughter because the expert witness said he could find no evidence of mental disease and the accused was as sane as you or I, we can't do a damn thing about it. That's what happened in Rex v Lee don't you remember Raynor?"

"I do indeed," said the Lord Chief Justice shaking his head. "When they say the law is an ass and you hear about cases like that you have to feel like agreeing with them. He was a naval chappie wasn't he? Why, his floosy packed him in even though he was leaving his wife and child, and so he strangled her. If that's not murder what is? That young fellow Denning, was the defence barrister, bit of a silver tongue if you ask me. He said the rogue, Lee, that was his name had had headaches. Good God! make that an excuse you would never hang anyone, it would be anarchy! That is the problem with juries they take more notice of a persuasive personality than the facts of the case."

The third Judge looked pensive. "If we sent it back to the jury, we could be said to be supporting the jury system while still upholding the strict letter of the law. It would be down to the jury to decide then. But is it legal?"

At this point Goddard stood up, "If we say it's legal it's legal and will remain so unless somebody appeals. The Prosecution are clearly not interested as they had nothing to say so it's hardly likely anyone would appeal it."

It was quickly agreed that the Appeal would be granted and that a re-trial should take place. Delegating a colleague to write the findings up, Goddard found his colleagues anxious that the Bench was not too critical of their brother Judge who it was agreed was "a good chap, usually very sound," and the third judge added, "I was in Chambers with his father." Hence, when the finding was eventually announced it boiled down to the fact that while he had given a very good and fair summation of both the facts and the law, he should have left the actual finding to the jury.

When he was informed of the Justices decision Mr Barratt replied that, "while thanking their honours for the offer of one there was no bail application as Mr O'Donnell said he was finding his cell an excellent retreat from the World." When he notified the court of his client's decision, his barrister did not use the Vicar's actual words to him which had included to "contemplate my sins which are many," in case someone took them to include a breach of the sixth commandment - thou shalt not kill.

Chapter Twenty Four

A date for Nurse Mackenzie

Perhaps it was a growing confidence in each other's company that caused Moira's second date with her new found boy-friend to be less cheerful than the first. Moira had vowed to herself that she would tell him of her intention to visit Mr Redpath in London, but conveniently never found quite the right moment to do so. She did though mention how the death of Miss Henderson was impacting on the community far more than she would have been expected.

"Firstly, there is the Church. The Congregation is down by about half and hardly anyone wants to come there to get married. All kinds of horrid rumours are flying around about the Church being cursed."

"Oh dear, perhaps I should reconsider coming to your Bell Ringers Group."

"Don't be silly there's no truth in them. They are so ridiculous. One says she was hit by a stone being dropped by the Devil like the Agglestone only smaller, and that the Devil did it to make the Vicar look responsible."

"What on earth is the Agglestone? Major Calley pointed it out to me when we were playing golf but whatever is it?"

"The story is that the devil was going to drop it on the spire at Salisbury Cathedral but got tired carrying it and decided to drop it on Corfe Castle instead."

"And still missed it by miles. How utterly ridiculous I have seen that Agg Agg, whatever stone something that big would have knocked a hole as big as a barn door in the roof."

"Yes, but this lady knew all about the Puckstone as well, that is much smaller."

"You don't really believe any of this do you?"

"Of course not."

"Then why go on about it?"

"I am just trying to show you how people think ridiculous things when they can't explain something. Thinking our Vicar is responsible is just as ridiculous."

Her companion smiled gently refilling her coffee. "You said you had heard two theories. If one was this silly story about stones dropping from the heavens what was the other one?"

"To me the other one is more believable. They think it was a maniac who hid himself and could strike again at any time. It has put off some of the ladies on the flower rota and, with Miss Henderson being gone already, sometimes nobody does it at all."

He shook his head "My, my who would have thought the death of one little old lady could have caused so much trouble. I suppose it's not having known her so well they didn't realise how much she still did. Still a maniac would not think about things like that so perhaps it could have been. Against that, I would have thought if it was a maniac that they would have struck again by now, and didn't you say nobody could have got in or out without being seen?"

"Yes, that's right. It's what has put the Vicar in the dock. People are very susceptible though and Old Tom, what he has said, has set a lot of tongues wagging."

A look of puzzlement that crossed the face of the man to whom the remarks were addressed. "Oh, what did he say?"

"He thinks he might have seen a figure coming out of the Vestry door, but he wasn't sure."

"Why didn't he say this in Court?"

"He had already made a statement that nobody could have got in or out without him seeing. He was afraid they would think he was making it up. Although he thought it was too short to be a Vicar, he thought he was wearing a surplice and was afraid it would only make things look worse for the Vicar and make people think he was going ga ga. Mind you with the jury having convicted the Vicar on the evidence they heard, perhaps he might reconsider."

Moira then went on to describe the situation with the Will. "The solicitors aren't keen on paying out until they know if the Vicar is to get any. It's Miss Standish at the Nursing Home I feel sorry for as she could sell up and retire, but until the estate is settled it's all up in the air. I think the way things stand Miss Henderson's shares will have to be sold and won't fetch much. If she had just been left shares, it would have been much easier." Hearing this her boyfriend, for as such she was now coming to regard him, looked genuinely upset.

"Let's leave it, shall we? I came here to have an enjoyable evening with an attractive young lady."

"Even if she doesn't look like a Burne-Jones painting?"

"Especially if she doesn't look like a Burne-Jones painting" he joked, and they both laughed.

After this the evening passed in a more light hearted and convivial note. Towards its end he raised the question of coming to a bell-ringing session. Moira was glad in a way that he had. When she had suggested it, she had been thinking about getting extra members but now realised with his not living locally it was a no no. Besides, how would he fit in with the group and how awkward would she feel about having him in the group. This meant that when he made the suggestion that they next meet not to ring bells but to play golf, she was cautious but not dismissive.

"It would not be much fun for you and no competition I would be hopeless," she warned.

"Nonsense that's why there is a handicapping system in golf. You could play against anyone in golf and still give them a game."

A few more questions and some enthusiastic responses soon convinced her to "give it a go" and she looked forward to a morning with him in the fresh air, although dismissive of his suggestion she could be the next Patty Berg - whoever she was.

The snug in the Travellers Return was slightly more crowded than usual. DCI Crawford had joined the bell ringers and having bought a round of drinks and seen them placed before people, Sergeant Brownlow explained. "I hope you won't mind, but Inspector Crawford asked me if he might come to our meeting and I will let him explain why."

"Thank you, George," I do not use ranks as I am here tonight as an ordinary citizen. My official role ended when I turned the papers over to the charging Inspector and solicitor but I would not like being responsible for a miscarriage of justice."

"Then you think our Vicar is innocent?" interrupted Moira.

"Not entirely but I certainly don't think it's manslaughter though. Whoever killed Miss Henderson, it was a very carefully planned and executed murder and, to be frank, I seriously doubt your friend the Vicar would have either the nerve or the brain for it. Had it not been for you lot it could well have been passed off as a normal death."

"So, our meddling has caused a lot of trouble and we should not have interfered," said Moira who was beginning to feel rather guilty.

"Not a bit of it. Had it not been for George contacting me Miss Henderson's murderer would have got away with it, they still might. No, you did absolutely the right thing. My hands are tied now though and I need your help."

"I'm sure I speak for all of us. We will all be glad to help and see the proper killer is convicted and Miss Henderson gets justice." It was Brownlow who spoke, but nods of agreement indicated he had guessed the mood of his fellow Bell-Ringers. "I'm not sure though what you want us to do?"

"Can you remember my saying that all the evidence was circumstantial but because The Vicar was the only one in a locked building and no one was seen going in or out and all the key holders were accounted for it had to be the Vicar?"

"You summarise the situation very well Inspector," chimed Daltry. It explains why I am not entirely convinced it was not the Vicar. I am never sure whether his bumbling attitude is genuine or not. Half the time I think he uses it as a defence mechanism to do nothing or get his own way without ruffling feathers."

"You may be right," agreed the Inspector, "but my theory falls down if there was someone in the church besides the Vicar, when Miss Henderson went in."

"If there were, then them is the one I saw walking through the graveyard."

Said old Tom.

"What! You never mentioned that in Court" objected the Inspector.

"I was afraid they would think I was making it up. In fact, I am half wondering now, if I dreamt it."

"People don't normally dream in colour Tom," said Moira and you mentioned a red beard, it was the only thing distinctive you could remember about the person."

"That's true, but I can't understand how I never saw no one afore I locked up. I always check and I does it carefully at that. Back when the War was on, poor old Mrs Henshaw was kneeling down in a pew, praying for her son what was away in Africa, and I missed her and she was locked in overnight. Ever since I always look up the bell tower, look all down each pew and stick me 'ead in the Vestry."

"That's fair enough," said Crawford, "but one thing I have realised reflecting on how it could possibly be anyone but the Vicar, is that the doors being locked would not maybe matter. You see the Vestry door is a Yale one. If a person was inside, they could just slip the latch and let themselves out. Is the door on the inside of the Vestry usually locked?"

"Oh no not since I ended up locking Mrs Henshaw in. She reckoned it made her arthritis play up for weeks and the Vicar had the lock on the inside door removed so people could get out through the Vestry door by making it a Yale lock. He said we are not so hard up for a congregation as to have to lock folks in."

"These are all things you can testify about at the new trial," said Crawford enthusiastically. "I think it will create enough doubt in the minds of the jury to secure an acquittal."

"That's as maybe," broke in Daltry, the solicitor, "but unless someone else is convicted, people will always be suspicious and it really won't look good for the church."

Crawford could not disagree with this but was afraid that, while technically the file on the murder would remain open, unless a similar murder took place the Chief Constable would soon have other cases to worry about, and that if the murderer was to be caught it would very much be down to the public and most specifically those sat round the table with him coming forward with information.

The assembled Bell-Ringers agreed that they would do what they could with more or less enthusiasm.

In fact, apart from Sergeant Brownlow who read through all the paperwork, nothing more was done by any of the group, except Nurse Mackenzie for whom the case was becoming an increasing interest. It had put her in touch with two very personable young men and if the fall out for the Vicar, who even if innocent, was looking distinctly less positive, she felt she should do all she could to unmask the killer of poor old Miss Henderson returned to her, as it was not considered value in the case of the Vicar, but for Moira it was a matter of nagging concern as to whether her suggestion that the date had been forged was correct. She decided to investigate She had had the bill for the breakfast over which she had raised a query further.

To this end, and to it fitting in with her shift pattern she returned to the Barrington Hotel in which it had been issued on a Tuesday. Having parked her Morris-Traveller, she went in and ordered tea and toast, looking around to see if she could see anything of note while she waited for her food to arrive. When it did, she asked the middle aged, grey- haired lady, who served her, if Friday was her regular work day. It was fortunate that there was only one other occupied table, where a couple were engaged in consuming their meal and reading the papers, for the waitress was of the friendly chatty sort who readily responded. "Yes, love as well as every Tuesday not to mention Monday, Wednesday and Thursday. I don't work at the weekend as my old man likes me at home and on Saturdays I does the shopping."

"So would you have been working here in April this year?"

"This year, last year and going back twenty years when old Mr Hawkes was the owner."

"In that case can I show you something." Nurse Mackenzie opened her hand bag and took out the bill, which she had carefully slipped inside an envelope and passed it across to the waitress.

The waitress, whose name was Myrtle, peered at the piece of paper holding it at arms length. Moira quickly saw this was due not to fear of it, but in order to focus on what was written on it. "Can't see a lot wrong with it. Oh yes, bacon and eggs it must have been served before half ten. It all goes back to old Mr Hawkes. He said that we was a restaurant not a greasy spoon cafe. People having bacon it would not smell right and would put off other diners. He's been gone for years but we have always kept the rule."

"Can I ask you about the date? What do you think it says?"

"Oh, I'm sorry my dear my eyes are not up to seeing fine print, but it's definitely my writing a large B & E that's how I always writes it when they order that."

Worryingly, Moira began to think she might have been right in thinking the date had been changed. Seeking confirmation she asked "I think you said you don't work on Saturday's though."

"That's right, why when do you think it was?"

"It's a bit unclear whether it was the 11th April or the 17 admitted Moira. That's a Saturday or a Friday."

"Well," said the waitress, "there ain't a problem it must have been Friday cos I don't work on a Saturday and then there's my initials MW, Myrtle Watkins."

"I don't suppose you can remember anything about the person who ordered it?"

"Come on love it was months ago and I ain't no memory-man. Mind you there are not too many as comes in here and has bacon and eggs. Most who are that way inclined have the full English. Hang on my dear, there was one Saturday in April I did work. One of the temporary girls had a friend who was getting married and her were a bridesmaid. That would have been around that time. And that morning we had three as all ordered bacon and eggs."

"One of them wasn't a young chap with a garish sweater was it?" asked Moira fearing the answer would be a positive one."

"Oh no love, not if I'm thinking of the right week. There was what I call a city gent in a suit but it was one of the others as I remember most. He was an old gentleman. I tell you why I remembers him. He kept his hat on all the time. It seemed a bit odd. I mean ladies do, like that Isobel Barnett. You wouldn't give a lady with a hat on a second thought "tis only polite and gentile, but a chap. It's not like it was cold neither." He had glasses and a beard and bent over his food like he was having trouble seeing it."

A weight lifted from Moira's mind. She could have been right in thinking the date was forged but clearly it was not Oliver Henderson. Three people ordering the same meal? Was that suspicious. Perhaps George Brownlow was on the right track in thinking there was a conspiracy to get the Nursing home land developed. She left a generous tip when she left and began the drive back to the Isle of Purbeck in a relieved frame of mind.

It was only as she drove through Wareham that she thought. If I was right, and the bill was for a breakfast on Saturday and had been altered how come it was in the pocket of a younger man who had had his breakfast there on Friday? Her fear that Miss Henderson's nephew had gone there on a Saturday to give himself an alibi for Friday had to be wrong, unless he had an accomplice or somebody else was trying to implicate him by making it look as if he had cooked up a false alibi, but who? Her mind went back to what Inspector Crawford had said about if Miss Henderson was murdered about the murder being carefully planned and executed. Would not such a person be capable of cleverly framing another person who had a motive?

Chapter Twenty Five

A search and a plan

That evening, she met up with Sergeant Brownlow in the Travellers. It had been agreed as a rendezvous for any bell ringers who had turned up anything in their investigations. Notably Moira and the Sergeant were the only two there. A momentary resentment that Moira had made the trip to the restaurant without him soon vanished, with the realisation how difficult it was for two people with full time jobs to carry out an investigation.

"Well, it's interesting that the waitress confirms she wrote it, but the dating of it could still have been forged. That is some progress," observed the Sergeant. "It sounds like the person who got it wanted to hide their identity."

"I know and it's a bit of a comfort to know it was an old man not a young one, but it still doesn't explain how it came to be in Olly's, I mean Mr Henderson's pocket."

"Did the waitress indicate if this elderly man had a beard?"

"No, I suppose I should have asked." Moira shook her head, a fine detective she was proving. "Are you thinking that the man who got the bill on Tuesday could be the same man that old Tom saw in the graveyard on Friday? Why if it was, he could have put it in Olly's pocket to frame him."

"A possibility I grant you, but it's taken a couple of long shots together. Besides, when would this chap with the beard have had the opportunity to put it in Mr Henderson's pocket? Now don't take this the wrong way, but I thought we ought to see if we can trace this beard."

"So, you think it was Olly. You are just as bad as the people who think it was the Vicar. You are putting two and two together and making six," she fumed.

"Not at all. You have to go where the evidence leads you and it can end up helping to lift suspicion. I must admit I did wonder if, given that he was involved with the Dramatic Society at Oxford, your Mr Henderson might have taken one, so I got my old colleague to make a few enquiries with that Don fellow who was involved with them. It turns out they thought one had gone missing."

Moira's face had gone pale. Could it be that the red bearded figure in the graveyard could have been the murderer leaving the scene of his crime?

Then Sergeant Brownlow's face creased in a smile. "It turns out it hadn't", he said. Tt should have been returned to the Costume people but it turned up in a box with all the props from a production that he was in. Evidently, he had been in such a hurry to get a drink after the last night that he slapped it down on the props table and went to the Bird and Baby dressed in his costume but without his beard! It threw me as I have never heard of a pub with that name, but apparently it's the nickname of the Eagle and Child which is a pub just down the road from the Playhouse in Oxford.

Moira's momentary relief was soon overshadowed by another thought. "Then was old Tom wrong when he thought he saw a figure with a red beard?"

"Not necessarily. There are more red beards than one floating about and more people than Mr Oliver Henderson who could have been wearing them. I think we should make a thorough search of the area that Tom was talking about. I know it was a month or two ago but a beard wouldn't rot and if we can find the beard it will probably not help us in learning who wore it but it will give weight to old Tom's testimony.

The next evening by the time they had finished work there were still a couple of hours of daylight left so they met up at the church gate and followed a path down past the back of the church in to the graveyard.

"Surely if it had been left here someone should have seen it and handed it or thrown it away by now." suggested Moira.

"I agree," responded George. "It would have had to be put under cover and I really can't see anywhere in the graveyard where he could have hidden it. I think it's more likely he got over the fence into the farmyard and put it in there somewhere."

Moira's nurse's uniform was not really designed for clambering over dry stone walls, but George gently lifted her over the dry-stone wall that separated the church from the farmyard next door, before scrambling over it himself. First, they searched an open sided barn that was used as a cattle shelter in winter, but was at present unoccupied. Starting at opposite ends they searched carefully, looking in and under buckets and sifting carefully from the straw scattered on parts of the barn floor, without success. They then tackled the outside of the yard. Moira was going through the inside of a wheel-less car abandoned in the yard, while George inspected an old tractor which, to judge by its rusty condition, had been out of action for years. Looking into the exposed engine, he made a discovery. "My word, look what we have here."

Moira screwed her head round from the inside of the car. "Is it the beard?"

"No, but it is just as helpful in backing up Tom's story. It's a surplice so Tom was right about that. Strange, you would have thought if he had time to get out of the surplice, he would have hidden the beard as well."

Moira looked thoughtful. "I'm not so sure. You are right. It would have been a lot easier just to get rid of the beard, unless it was glued on. But leaving the surplice here meant if it was found it might be seen as evidence against the Vicar. I am just getting more and more confused. It's so much easier being a nurse. Your job must be awfully difficult."

"What makes you say that Moira? I've always enjoyed it."

"Nurses deal with drugs you know what they are going to do, but people are so unpredictable and you can end up being suspicious of the nicest of people"

"Are you thinking about what's happening to the Vicar?"

"Partly, but this breakfast receipt was even making me suspicious of Oliver."

"I can't see that. Why, surely it gives him a cast iron alibi."

"That is one way of looking at it, but if I am right in thinking that the date on it was forged and it was actually issued on a Saturday, then whoever did it was manufacturing an alibi and is the guilty person. Although whether they manufactured the alibi for themselves or to make someone else look guilty, who knows."

"In that case my money would be on someone else. If it was that Oliver Henderson, why did he not produce the bill the first time he was interviewed? When he did find it, it was only an afterthought that it had to be issued before ten thirty because of what he ate."

"I'm glad to hear you say that. It makes me a lot happier about an idea I am going to suggest, which I think could unmask the killer."

"How on earth can we do that?" asked Brownlow.

"Let's write a list of all the suspects we can think of. Then we send a type written note to them all saying we know who did it and to meet somewhere with some money, if they want us to keep quiet."

George rubbed his chin. "It's certainly a thought. It might work. Heaven knows what DCI Crawford would say. He'd blow a gasket. If the police did that, it would be seen as entrapment."

"But it wouldn't be the police it would be me. My first thought was that the only person who the murderer would suspect had information would be old Tom, but there is no way I would risk putting him in harm's way. Then I thought if I mention the fact that I saw somebody in the church and have something they left behind but for £200 I could lose it and forget, someone might take the bait."

"The bait I take it being you. You are playing with fire here Moira. If the murderer does turn up, they might bring the money but, equally, they might come to kill you. Someone who has killed once usually finds it easier to kill again." There followed an intense argument but finally Sergeant Brownlow agreed to help put the plan in to operation with two provisos. The first was that he tell his wife Mary and got her blessing and the second that Nurse Mackenzie left a sealed envelope for the police with a trusted friend, in case things went wrong.

That night Moira typed out five identical letters with the exception that while indicating the same day and meeting place the times were spaced at twenty minute intervals coinciding with Ferry departure times. They read

I FOUND SOMETHING IN THE CHURCH
YOURS FOR £100
OR WOULD YOU RATHER HANG FOR MURDER?
I SAW YOU!

Board the Sandbanks Ferry at.   on foot with the money

One who wishes you well

She waited for a phone call from the Brownlows' residence, where that evening a conversation had taken place between George and

Mary consuming their main course of Shepherd's Pie and their sweet. Unusually for him, George opened a second bottle of beer and shared it out between the two glasses on the table. He had explained to his wife about the conversation and the argument he had had with Moira and how he had agreed to go along with her suggestion provided he had his wife's blessing. He was looking into his glass and avoiding eye contact as he said, "If Moira was willing to risk her neck, I am willing to risk mine, but I can't risk my police pension without your agreement."

His wife smiled and reached across the table to hold his hand. "You are such a good man George. You help others without any thought of yourself. Of course, you go ahead. I can happily live without your pension as long as I had you."

Still staring intently into his beer glass, George, who found it difficult to show emotion, smiled and said "I thought you would see it that way old girl"

"Not so much of the old," she retorted withdrawing her hand and giving him a playful slap. "One other thing I could live without your pension but If anything happened to you,"

She paused before adding "Who on earth would eat my jam roly poly?

"Eating jam roly poly is that all I'm good for?"

As in all the best relationships love and humour were not far apart. "That and one or two other things," she smiled and winked.

Chapter Twenty Six

Folly on the Ferry

The next morning Moira fulfilled the other condition George had put on to his agreement to participate, in the scheme to unmask the killer. Her morning calls had taken her to Convent where she had to change the dressing on the ulcerated leg of one of the Sisters. Before she left, she knocked on the door of the Mother Superior with a request that she should give a letter she handed to her to anyone in authority if they requested it. She readily agreed, glad of the opportunity to be of service to the nurse, who was a frequent visitor and who was so highly thought of by the sisters.

Nurse Mackenzie had chosen the Sandbanks Ferry remembering it from her schoolgirl days on holiday. The company which introduced it was set up in 1926 using a boat built on the Isle of Wight. Having driven to the ferry together, she remembered her father buying shares in it as they used it on holiday and how he had been engrossed in the court case between the ferry Company and the Davis brothers who saw it encroaching on their passengers only service. Moira and George bought their tickets and took up their positions on the ferry. Both were on the upper pedestrian deck on the seaward side of the vessel. Moira had situated herself facing out to sea about halfway along, while George waited near the boarding end and scanned the passengers walking on board. The crossing took about ten minutes and the ferry always left the Sandbanks side at ten minutes to, ten minutes past and on the half hour. Thus, expecting the suspects to come from the Swanage side, the first suspect's letter had contained the time of 2.00p.m.

George was vigilant knowing that while Miss Henderson's murderer might just come with the ransom money, he might intend to ensure Nurse Mackenzie's silence in a far more permanent manner. He felt he really should have said to Moira about a ferry being all too convenient a spot to tip somebody over board. On the other hand there would be plenty of witnesses and escape would not be easy. When the Ferry's engines kicked into life and the chains began to clank, no sign of the suspect, who had been allotted the first time, Doctor Carrington, was to be seen so George moved to the far end of the ferry so he could observe if anyone boarded at the other end of the crossing. George repeated the process at the times allotted to the second and third suspects. Again, he saw no one. Moira was beginning to think what had seemed such a good idea, when it first came into her head, was beginning to fear it was going to be a waste of time. George, knowing who the third suspect was, was in a particularly relaxed frame of mind. He carefully observed the passengers whether they were walking on or pushing a bike, but saw no sign of the respected figure who had received the third letter.

As the ferry neared mid channel, a figure darted up the steps dropped a rolled up newspaper over Moira's shoulder and disappeared back down the stairs whence he had come. Moira opened the newspaper and cried out, "It's worked," "seeing a wad of rolled up bank notes. One or two people looked round in surprise and a young girl clutched her doll in fright, but George Brownlow was the only one to move. Mortified that, somehow, he had missed the suspect and fearing his inattentiveness had left Moira in danger, he raced to her side. She assured him she was alright and urged him to get after the man who had vanished as quickly as he had appeared. Calling out to Moira to wait for him by the Haven Hotel, he sped down the steps towards the car deck cursing that he had not imagined any suspect would have disregarded the instruction to come on foot. He struggled to get between the cars and checked their occupants and before he had finished, the safety gates were hauled back. Thinking it was possible that the man he was looking for might have concealed himself somewhere on the Harbour side of the vehicles, he set to searching there. Engrossed in his search he failed to notice the ferry had begun its return trip and realised he would have to wait for the next crossing to get back to Moira and confirm that suspect number three had taken the bait.

Moira had sat down on a bench on the quayside in front of the Haven hotel. Her feelings were a combination of amazement and relief. Amazement that respected solicitor, Rotarian and church warden, Archibald Daltry should be revealed as the murderer and relief that it was not a younger man, who she was increasingly beginning to feel she was falling in love with. She guessed her policeman friend had been trapped on the ferry having failed to get ashore and settled down to await the ferry's return. Only a couple of minutes spent wondering what on earth had prompted Archibald Daltry to become a killer when what looked like a police car with a blue light on top drew up. A man got out and approached her.

"Can you tell me what you have got there?" he asked, pointing at the newspaper on her lap."

"Are you a police officer?" she responded.

"I am," confirming it with a warrant card which he pulled from his pocket.

"In that case I had better tell you that this is blackmail money and that I was given it by a local solicitor."

At this point the police officer interrupted her and said "Don't say anything else. Can you be kind enough to step over to that car." He pointed to the police vehicle drawn up a few yards away

No sooner had she complied than he called to his uniformed colleague in the car asking him to join them. He turned back to her and said "I am arresting you on suspicion of demanding money with menaces you are not obliged to say anything but anything you do say may be taken down and given in evidence."

"But it was a trap my policemen friend helped me," she cried.

"In that case I had better tell you that you could be charged with conspiracy as well as blackmail."

Almost before she knew it the uniformed officer who had emerged from the car pulled her wrists together and slapped on a pair of handcuffs. The plain clothed officer bundled her in to the back of the police car which headed off back towards Canford Cliffs and Poole Police Station.

A few minutes later a bewildered George Brownlow was looking frantically for any sign of Moira but finding none decided to return to the ferry on the off chance that any other suspect who had been sent a letter showed up. He realised it was unlikely as it seemed they had flushed out the murderer, or at least an accomplice, but felt there was little else he could do.

The reason two of the suspects had not turned up was due to events earlier that morning. Coming off duty, at mid-day, a breathless and agitated Miss Standish had arrived at Doctor Carrington's house. Taking her through to his private quarters he settled her down on the settee and placing a comforting arm around her shoulders, asked what the problem was.

"It's this," she said opening the catch of her handbag and took out an envelope which had been opened. She handed it to Doctor Carrington looking at him with terrified eyes. She was initially bemused, but almost instantly enraged when he burst out laughing.

The Doctor's reaction was explained when he went to his desk and pulling out a similar envelope flourished it in the air with one word "Snap!"

Chapter Twenty Seven

Sorting out a muddle

It was largely due to the efficiency of the Poole police that Nurse Mackenzie was spared a night in jail. That the aforementioned police had not thought much of her attempt to discover Miss Henderson's murderer was shown by the fact that, while one police car had fetched George Brownlow and another had checked to find that what Nurse Mackenzie had said about her contacting other suspects was true when she was released from custody she and George Brownlow were left to catch a bus home. Sergeant Brownlow had received something of a dressing down from the custody Sergeant at Poole.

The journey home was a tearful one on the part of Nurse Mackenzie who wept copiously. This was partly the result of the shock of being arrested and partly as a result of the embarrassment she had caused George.

"I am so sorry I dragged you in to this Sergeant," she sobbed.

"I have to agree but, for goodness sake, call me George. I didn't agree to this because you are a District Nurse or because I am a policeman but because you are a friend and a jolly good one at that." Looking out across Studland as the bus took them home the pair reflected on the day's events. "I would not have minded being arrested if I felt we had achieved something. Still, I suppose we have eliminated Archibald as a suspect."

"Maybe," was the Sergeant's non committal response.

"Oh, come on George surely you don't think somebody who had done the murder would have gone to the police?"

"You are probably right but if he was convinced no one had seen him or could identify him being in the church it would strengthen his position. He has certainly cleared himself in your eyes. To be honest in mine too. He would never have the bottle to carry out a murder never mind going to the police about a blackmailer who'd seen him."

By the time the bus passed through Studland, Moira's spirits were reviving somewhat and her mind was returning to her apparently failed attempt of the afternoon. "You are sure George that neither of the last two people I sent letters to turned up?"

"I don't think so. With you having disappeared I hung around but did not see either of the people who had the notices you sent."

"What if more than one person is involved? Perhaps I am clutching at straws but might that not be the case if what you found out about the building application is true. I mean there must be a lot of money involved and some people are ruthless."

"It is a possibility but not a very likely one. It is much easier to get planning permission by dropping some money in the right people's pockets than risking getting hung for murder. To my mind, it is more likely if two people were involved and both got your ransom note, they would realise it was a hoax."

As they got off the bus and went their separate ways home George uttered a final word of warning "Best to leave things alone. I am sure they will all turn out alright in the end."

When he got home, his wife, Mary informed him that Roger Crawford had rung and she suggested it would be wise to phone him before he had his supper.

Doing as suggested, he had only got half way through saying he was returning the call before the voice on the phone exploded with such vehemence that he held the ear piece away.

"George Brownlow, what on earth were you thinking about? You could have got yourself and Miss Mackenzie killed, never mind finding yourself on disciplinary proceedings for entrapment."

"I know Sir. I am sorry Sir."

"So am I George but not for the reason you imagine."

"What is that Sir?"

"Because I don't know if I would have done the same myself, but I know that I should have."

"I have to disagree with you there, Sir. You have always been a model policeman and done things by the book."

"But why George? To advance my career? Get a conviction? I passed the buck on this one and if your Mr O'Donnell hangs, I will never forgive myself, because it will be my fault."

"No Sir, with respect, it will be his own fault because he is too pig headed to tell a lie. He would no more have killed Miss Henderson than I would. He would only have to say he can't remember locking the door and no jury on earth would convict him. An open door would have meant someone else could have been in the church."

"That is the problem. What sort of system of justice relies on somebody needing to tell lies. When I was a young PC, I spoke to an old lady who had lived in Lancashire and been on the force. She resigned because her boss fitted a villain up by planting a gun in his house. Noble cause corruption they called it because they knew he was guilty but could not prove it. The trouble is I am beginning to think that I know O'Donnell is not the murderer but I can't prove it."

"Proving a negative is never easy Sir, that's why Nurse Mackenzie and myself are trying so hard to prove who did do it."

"Well good luck, but be careful. You know my hands are tied. All I can do is go over my evidence and make sure, when the re-trial comes, I turn up anything that can be said in your Vicar's favour."

Chapter Twenty Eight

Archibald's Apology

If many people were being caused continuing distress by the on-going question of who had killed Miss Henderson, the Landlord of the Travellers was certainly benefitting from the meetings of the Bell Ringers which had always been held only once a month and were now becoming an almost weekly occurrence. This one began with Archibald Daltry admitting he owed Miss Mackenzie an apology or, at least, an explanation of why she had been arrested.

"It is my fault she was arrested and had the indignity of being handcuffed. I don't feel though I have not been true to my Rotary Pledge. It all began you see at a Rotary meeting in Bournemouth, a member, whose name is not important, being aware that the Nursing Home was in financial difficulties had told a couple of other members, possibly in violation of his professional ethics, but in my book entirely compliant with the four-way test, and suggested a way in which they might be able to help. As a result, one of our builder members made a planning application using the advice of Mr Ramsey, one of our estate agent members, as to what would sell and what would produce a good price, and put in the provisional application. You see, once planning permission was granted, the bank would be quite happy to grant a much larger overdraft, because they had the security of the land value if they went into administration or were declared bankrupt. Now, those of you who know me, and I like to think you all do, will know that I will always tell the truth," 'often at all too great a length,' thought Moira as he continued. "I must admit that I gave the project my full support. Partly because I had been promised all the legal work for my firm, but also because I believed it was not only fair, but beneficial to all concerned."

"And I am sure you were right Sir," agreed George Brownlow hoping he had finished.

He was wrong, however for Archibald Daltry continued "I may be happy to benefit from something that is mutually beneficial, but not if it involves murder. I began to fear that I was being dragged in to something with which I had no desire to be involved. It was one of the reasons I persuaded the Vicar to appeal. I wanted the truth, whatever it was, to come out. In my book murder is never justified, even if it agrees with the four-way test. Hence, when it seemed someone suspected my involvement and had sent me a blackmail note I went to the police in Bournemouth. They felt the information should not be shared with their colleagues in Swanage, just in case of corruption within that police force, but asked me to comply with the requirements of the blackmailer while they kept watch."

At this point he hung his head "You see, I did not realise it was you who sent the note. If I had I like to think I would have realised it was a hoax."

"No need to apologise Archie old bean." Olly has really got in my head thought Moira, I'm even talking like him. Acting like Olly as well as talking like him, him she slapped him on the back and said "No hard feelings. I'll get you another."

The combination of being bought a drink by a woman and having a second small sherry was enough to cause Archibald to fall silent.

Archibald's Apology

Moira Mackenzie extended her invitation to the rest of the bell ringers and for once they all responded positively with more than one thinking if a woman could be allowed to buy a round of drinks and show such determination and ingenuity, even if unsuccessfully to bring about a just ending, why could she not be a Rotarian?

Chapter Twenty Nine

A visit to Old Harry

The phone call that had been made to Moira that same evening turned out not to be from a patient, but to her delight from Oliver Henderson. He had announced he was coming down at the next weekend to sort out some stuff from his Aunt's house and would she like to meet up. Moira readily agreed and they decided that he would ring again the day before coming down and they would decide what to do and where to meet depending on the weather.

"I'll look forward to it," he said, "that is unless I have been arrested."

"Whatever for?" she asked.

"Why murder, but then you don't know do you. I had this letter somebody trying to blackmail me, saying they had found something in the church."

She laughed "Oh, I shouldn't worry about that several people had them."

"That's a relief then, but how do you know?"

"It's too complicated to explain on the phone. I will tell you when I see you."

"That's fair enough old sport. Toodle pip."

The conversation had been short but long enough to set Nurse Mackenzie thinking about the murder again. That he had not turned up and acceded to the blackmail threat yet seemed perfectly happy to talk about it was reassuring. He clearly thought he might be arrested, but the fact that he was coming down seemed to imply that he realised he was not guilty, and she was pleased she seemed to have set his mind at rest.

With the matter back in her head, it set her to mentally tick off the people that had received the hoax letter.

Mrs Hinton – hardly likely to be a murderer and if she had dropped something in the church it would not be surprising, as she was in there most weeks.

Miss Standish – She was much more rarely in church, so something like a glove with forensic evidence on it would look highly suspicious.

Doctor Carrington - He had been to the church to try to treat Miss Henderson, so again, something of his would not be that incriminating.

Archibald - she had already dismissed , him as hardly having the nerve to tip of the police if he actually was the murderer.

Her Olly, as she was beginning to regard him, seemed unconcerned, it must have been a relief to him the letter was a hoax as she was certainly unaware of him being in church recently, if ever.

She began to wonder. If the Vicar hadn't done it, and none of the people she had sent notes to, who could it be? Suddenly she thought - Old Tom. Perhaps being so familiar had blinded her. Nobody in their right mind would have murdered Miss Henderson, she was such a harmless old lady. She remembered the words of DCI Crawford – that the person who did it was very lucky or very cunning! Was anyone who killed another human being ever in their right mind? Tom Watkins had been through some awful experiences in the trenches, had that unhinged him in some way? She remembered Major Calley talking about a couple of elephants that had gone berserk when he was out in India. It turned out they had both seen members of their herd slaughtered when they were younger. Had something Miss Henderson had done that morning triggered something in poor old Tom's head and caused him to act like those elephants?

An evening phone call on Friday saw Oliver Henderson agreeing to meet Moira on Saturday afternoon. He was going to be down in Purbeck early Saturday morning but, with things to tidy up at his Aunt's house, it was agreed they would meet up in the afternoon. Moira's spirits had lifted and she felt she now had a plausible alternative suspect to the vicar.

When Oliver Henderson rang her, she intimated this fact to him.

"The thing is Olly I think I know who did it, not that I will tell anyone, until I have checked a couple of things. I don't want to end up making a fool of myself like I did with the ferry business. Mind you I think it's only a matter of time before they confess, at least, I hope so."

"Oh, yes – so do I, you will have to tell me all about it tomorrow."

"Never mind that where are we going to meet? Do you want to go to the golf club again?"

"Best not, no offence but you are still a bit of a novice and it might cause delays on a busy Saturday. How about going up on the cliffs above Old Harry there is plenty of space there and I can put some clubs and a stack of balls in for you to have a practice? I aim to make you the next Patty Berg."

When she got in her Morris Traveller, to drive from Lyddcastle to the Old Harry Cliffs. Moira was in a happy mood. She had attended all her morning calls in Swanage and Corfe, with no unforeseen problems and had a warm welcome from her patients for many of whom she was as much a friend as a nurse. Arriving home she had changed out of her uniform and put on a pleated tartan skirt that she felt comfortable playing golf in. The hemline was just below the knee thus showing off her legs, which she always felt were her best feature without exposing the scar on her knee. The morning had been fine and after a brief scud of rain the blue sky and sunshine very much matched her mood.

The Old Harry Cliff Top had not been a place she had much enjoyed going as a child on holiday. Her parents telling her that Old Harry was a nickname for the Devil, she remembered, as she had as a nine year old burst in to tears when she had heard how Old Harry had lost his wife in 1896 when she had fallen in to the sea. She laughed inwardly remembering how she had thought his wife was an actual person who had fallen off the cliff top rather than a chalk stack that collapsed into the sea. Now she dismissed all the stories about the devil, thinking the story about it being a pirate called Harry hiding his ship behind the rocks before attacking passing ships as a much more likely story.

A tractor and trailer had been a minor annoyance as she was held up behind them for a period. It was a common occurrence in the area but she thought it was a small price to pay for living in such a beautiful area of the country, free from any smoke and grime. Anyway, she mused, being a few minutes late would do no harm, as it would certainly do no harm to Olly to wait for a few minutes.

Coming to the crest of the downs she saw Olly's car in the distance. The dry weather and chalk soil meant there was no problem in driving off the road across the grass and, seeing that this is what Olly had done, she did the same, pulling up a few yards short of the cliff edge. She got out and was surprised to see the driver's side door of the other car had been left open and that the key was in the ignition. She approached cautiously, half expecting that Olly would have concealed himself and would pop up in one of his silly pranks to which he was inclined. Nothing happened and she began to sense something was wrong. She looked hopefully in all directions. The barren cliff top afforded an unobstructed view in all directions, but she could see no sign of movement. She quickened her pace as she walked all around the car but saw nothing except a couple of envelopes lying on the driver's seat.

She lent in and saw that one of the envelopes was addressed with the one word, MOIRA. Realising this must be her, she snatched it up and tore it open.

Chapter Thirty

Revelations

Inside it she read the following

> Dear Moi,
>
> If you are reading this it means I have had the courage to do the right thing. I was going to drive over the cliff edge in Gertie, but the old girl never did anything wrong. It also means I can leave it to you, if the authorities will take this as my last will and testament. Hope it shows there are no hard feelings, quite the reverse. I enjoyed our short time together and would not have changed it for the World. Shall we meet again? Who knows?
>
> Ollie

Moira was tempted to open the second envelope, which was addressed to the Swanage Police Authority. Would she have wanted the envelope addressed to her opened by anyone else? No, she thought, so slipped it into her hand bag and drove away.

She had been looking forward to a carefree afternoon swinging a golf club. Now it seemed the person she had intended to spend it with was dead. Fighting to hold back the tears, she tried desperately to keep her mind on her driving as she made her way to the home of George Brownlow. Olly had wanted the Dorset police to have the letter but was not George a member of the force.

When George opened his door, she burst out "Oh George, I am so glad you are in. I think you should have this."

"Come in, come in," said George seeing her distressed state "Here you had better come and sit down."

No sooner had she done so that Mary Brownlow poked her head round the door and seeing Moira's distressed state said "I think a cup of strong tea is called for."

When George asked her what the matter was, she explained how she had come by it and proffered the note that had been addressed to her. "I was late. If only I had been on time, I could have told him we sent several people the note. He must have thought I knew he was the murderer and now he is dead and it is all my fault."

"Hold your horses Moira, if he did commit suicide, which on the face of this note looks likely but, by no means certain, we have no idea why he did it."

"What other reason could there be?" argued a bemused Moira.

"Perhaps this letter will tell us."

"Aren't you going to open it then?"

Before George could respond Mary emerged from her kitchen carrying a tray of tea and cakes. She set it down on the table and seeing Moira's distress placed a comforting arm round her shoulder.

"I'm sorry Moira," explained George, but I think in the circumstances it would be safest for everyone if I waited until I had another officer here, preferably one considerably higher ranking than myself. It should probably be finger printed."

"But why," cried Moira, "isn't it obvious given there was one for me as well and what it says?"

"You said you were afraid he may have thought you believed he murdered Miss Henderson, but he hadn't."

"I know, that is why it's so awful. I had told him on the phone I thought I knew who murdered Miss Henderson but had not said who I thought it was. I was going to explain it has struck me it had to be Old Tom."

"But have you considered the possibility that your Mr Henderson actually did murder Miss Henderson?"

Moira stared in to her half drunken cup of tea. Afraid to look anyone in the eye. She had considered it, all too often, but always managed to convince herself it was not true.

In the absence of a reply, George continued, "Motive, means, he was clearly strong enough and if he was in the church, opportunity. He could have been the person that Old Tom thinks he may have seen."

"How can he have been. He was having breakfast miles away. The receipt he had proves it"

"But you yourself spotted that it it could be a forgery because of the date being altered. In which case, it strongly suggests he was looking to create an alibi, and why do that unless you had done it."

Crestfallen, Moira's head sank down towards her chest, "I suppose I knew it could be him but I just did not want to believe it."

Mary used the arm that was wrapped around Moira to give her a comforting shake, "There, there dear, you won't be the first female taken in by a smooth- talking man. It's not my place, but I could have told you George, you should read more Agatha Christie. It's nearly always the person with an unbreakable alibi who did it."

"Why didn't you tell us love?" complained George.

"Would you have believed me? No. George would have listened to his head and you dear would have listened to your heart."

Much as he loved his wife, who could read him like a book, George knew the resolution to whether what she was saying was a wise observation or a reader's fantasy, lay within the envelope which remained unopened. Picking it up he went out to the hall and the telephone. On getting through to the station, the Desk Sergeant seemed unwilling to give him access to a high- ranking officer, until he told him it was about the O'Donnell case. This brought about an immediate change "In that case," said the Sergeant, "I must put you through to the Chief Constable. He is most concerned about it."

The Chief Constable was delighted to be able to redirect his attention from trying to boost tickets for the police Charity Ball to what he considered real police work. When his conversation with Geore Brownlow had finished, the latter was relieved that his contacting a high-ranking officer had been welcomed but worried that, within half an hour, his own house would be playing host to the Head of the Dorset Constabulary.

It turned out that not only the Chief Constable, but PC Ted Egan, who had driven him and WPC Jackson, the forces loan female officer, who had been brought in in case a female needed to be arrested or, more likely, given support. The Chief felt it was important that if women were going to be brought in to the force they should be entrusted with more than just making tea but was not quite willing to regard them as being equal to their male colleagues.

With the three females squeezed together on the sofa and Brownlow and the Chief Constable ensconced in armchairs, the seating capacity of the Brownlow's sitting room was exhausted, so Ted Egan was standing awkwardly in front of the fireplace.

"Any objection if I smoke Mrs Brownlow?" intoned the Chief Constable.

"Having received permission, he looked up and said "Very well Egan if you will be kind enough to open the envelope and read any contents. Can I ask …." Public School and the RAF had not really taught the Chief Constable how to deal with or address females, who he found a charming but distracting addition to the forces of law and order so that the instruction "To take notes if you would be so kind" was indicated by a wave of his pipe rather than a name or title.

Had he been asked to deal with a ticking time bomb, Egan could hardly have looked more worried. Steeling himself, he slid a finger nail in to the envelope and drew out a piece of paper, which he unfolded and read to the assembled company. WPC Jackson took out her police note book, but wondered what on earth for, if what her colleague was saying was already written down. Hey ho, she thought, at least I am not being asked to make tea.

Egan began somewhat awkwardly given the terminology he was using to senior officers.

Well old beans, it seems you tumbled me in the end. Mind you, I was dashed unlucky. If it had not been for the busy body bell ringers, Aunt Em would not have suffered the indignity of a post mortem. Let's face it, she could not have had too long left and I gave her a quick and painless end. You see, I rang her the previous day and she had been on her high horse about mending my ways and showing a bit more interest in her. As I have said before, I could see her leaving my families money to a Cat's Home and decided she would have to go. For all my planning, I did wonder if I would have had the nerve to do it. I am sorry for the distress I caused. I had thought what difference would it make if an old biddy died a few years before her time. I had not realised the ramifications that it would have. I like to think I would have owned up if the Vicar was going to be hung, but we had not got to that point before I think you had realised I was the real killer. That Nurse Mackenzie was the sharp cookie who caught me. The breakfast receipt was a fail safe. In case they had a description of someone and thought it was me in disguise I would have used it, but as they didn't, I wasn't going to produce it had it not fallen out of my pocket. It was a bit of good fortune, or so I thought. It is no pleasure for me to have to say it but, if it had not been down to Nurse Mackenzie and her colleagues. How was I know she would spot I changed the date. If she hadn't I would not be where I am today. I was in the church all along. I must say how I managed to put up with an hour of solid ringing sounds. It seemed a lot longer for I had concealed myself in the pulpit and it was dashed uncomfortable and quite damaged my golf for days after. I heard everyone going out and the door shutting before taking a seat in a pew. I did not have long to wait before my Aunt came in. I had spoken to her on the phone and said I would be down about eleven, so she said it would be alright as she could go down to the Church by nine and be back. I had kept my head down as though I was praying and when I turned round, she had her head down over the font fiddling with some flowers. I seized the moment for if she had turned round, I wonder if I would have had the ability to do it face to face so grabbed her from behind and squeezed. It was so easy. I wished instantly I had not done it, partly hoping that she was just unconscious and not dead. I belted down the aisle in to the Vestry. I had bought a red beard in a costume shop in Oxford, but I was afraid my jacket or sweater might give me away. I grabbed some white garment hung on a peg and looked out of the Vestry door. Seeing that apart from some chap cutting the grass who looked engrossed in his work there was no one about, so I belted down the graveyard. I realised I had gone the wrong way to the churchyard gate and hopped over a fence. A detour round the back of some farm buildings, gave me the chance to ditch my disguise and bought me back to the main road. It looked like I had got away with it, so walked calmly back to the main road and drove off to some woodland where I pulled up to reflect on what I had done. God, if there is one, will know, I am telling the truth when I say my mind seemed to go blank, for the next thing I remember is being up by Cliff Top House and being surprised that my Aunt was not there! Yet how could she be if I had strangled her an hour or so earlier? I don't expect anyone to believe that, so I could only expect to face the hangman, which I do not intend to do so I am resolved to drive off the top of the cliffs as long as my nerve holds. Please give my apologies to the Vicar, I did not mean to cause him the indignity and suffering he has been subject to, which is something I never intended.

Chapter Thirty One

Wedding bells

If bells can sound joyful, the bells that rang out from the tower of St Anselm's would have been positively jubilant. The sun was shining and the local people had turned out in large numbers. When the bells had ceased and the organist's rendition of Mendelson's wedding march had ended, the priest who pronounced the opening words of the marriage service, was St Anselm's own John O'Donnell. A couple of weeks earlier on his release, he had returned to his Vicarage to be greeted by three parcels, all of which were found to contain candle snuffers, given by lady parishioners, to welcome him home, and Mrs Mannion. She had faithfully looked after the Vicarage in its occupant's absence and on the return of "his eminence" in the absence of a fatted calf, had made a pineapple upside down cake. It had sagged in the middle and the Vicar, on saying he only wanted a very small piece, was given two huge slabs.

Perhaps the Vicar's happiest moment had come the next evening when, hearing of his release, Jane Clayton arrived in the evening at the Vicarage. When the door opened, she had hugged the Vicar like a tearful mother who has just found their missing child. John O'Donnell managed to extricate himself and asked if she would like to help him consume the huge selection of salad and cold meats that Mrs Mannion had left in the fridge for him. When she accepted, he suggested they share a bottle of wine first. It was an impetuous decision as he realised he would have to use the wine he had brought for communion but knew he would be able to visit Sam Loxton's for another bottle next morning.

It was strange, that whereas Jane had come to the Vicar to be her confessor, now, in the practical, if not the Catholic sense she had become his. "It must be wonderful to be home after that terrible time in prison," Jayne enthused.

"Glad to be home and to enjoy the company of people like yourself yes but prison was not so terrible. It makes me more appreciative of home comforts but the prison staff were most kind and being on remand I was able to spend time in my own cell and meditate. I think it has made me a better person. I shall certainly try to be more sociable and less keen to jump to conclusions."

"You were always the last person to do that anyway. How do you feel about Henderson does your Christian sense of forgiveness extend to him? I am afraid I would gladly kill him myself for the trouble he caused you, never mind murdering Miss Henderson."

"Given he is apparently dead already you might have a job," chuckled the Vicar. "Sometimes good comes out of evil and I shall certainly be using some of Miss Henderson's money for church repairs in due course. No, I certainly pray for him or his soul. I like to think what happened on that cliff top was good over-coming evil. It seemed a strange place to meet. I do wonder if he had intended to push her over the cliff and say it was an accident but perhaps his conscience got the better of him. Anyway, he has gone now but this salad hasn't so let's tuck in."

If Jane Clayton ate rather more of the salad, her host consumed rather more of the wine. Over the meal the conversation was wide ranging and concerned as much about the village and the church as themselves. When they finished the Vicar cleared away the plates and opened a bottle of port and found a couple of cheeses in the larder which he laid out along with some biscuits in front of the sofa, to which they retired. After two glasses of port, they agreed that the Fete they would organize and fund a fete to raise funds for the orphan children, would be an adequate penance to cover any sins they might commit that evening, and after a third they both fell asleep.

It was five o'clock the next morning when John O'Donnell awoke to find his companion had gone. Pleased he would have three hours at least before Mrs Mannion arrived, he went to his desk to write a letter to Archibald Daltry. One of the things he had discussed with Jane the previous evening was how to deal with the problem of the nursing home. He was going to suggest that he thought there was a way in which he could get the Parish Council to agree to wave the Covenant by allowing redevelopment once all the current residents had died. The new National Health Service meant the home was not making money and its sale would be the only way for the shareholders to recover their investment for a lease on the land while the church could obtain some funds. Running the establishment during the life of the residents would enable the staff to have time to find alternative employment.

The approval of the suggestions in the letter the vicar duly wrote met with the approval and agreement of all the parties involved, not least Archibald Daltry who claimed that both as a Church Warden and a solicitor it had passed his Rotary Four Way Test. It had also met with the approval of the Doctor and Matron of the Nursing home, who were now about to embark on a different sort of partnership.

Hence it was these two, who now stood before the Reverend O'Donnell to be joined in holy matrimony, were observed by a tearful audience. While weddings are an occasion for lachrymosity, the tears are usually tears of happiness but for one witness to the proceedings, this was not the case. Silent tears rolled down the cheek of Nurse Mackenzie. How could she have become so infatuated with a man!? Not even a professional one, but one a few years her junior in age and totally irresponsible. It was the groom in the day's proceedings who had comforted her after the exposure of Miss Henderson's real killer. "No", Doctor Carrington had said. "whether it was the conflict between good and evil in one man's soul or a mere chemical imbalance of the brain, I would not care to judge, but what I will say is that it was the clearest case of schizophrenia I have ever seen. No wonder they thought he was a good actor, he really was two different people."

The murderer's old golfing partner, Major Calley, was seated towards the rear of the church, after his exertions on the bells. He would miss his rounds of golf with young Henderson. He really could not see this jovial young chap as a murderer. Then he remembered the elephants, and how his mother the wife of his old army colleague, had met her end in the Blitz when a bomb had struck the Café de Paris. How does a young boy cope with that and what effect must it have on his views of right and wrong? Strange he thought but turned his mind to happier thoughts. He was looking forward to making his first ever appearance in the Isle of Purbeck mixed greensomes. His new golfing partner was seated further forward in the Church, crying like so many women do at a wedding.

Soon the congregation would be emptying, so this lady took out her compact and powdered dry the tears. Never again she vowed. She looked forward to growing old as a spinster, respected in her village where her many friends and patients would be more than compensation for what she had lost. To this church, this village and these people she would give years of faithful service. First though, she had a promise to keep and a visit to London to make. There she would get to judge the performance of a young barrister and find out what a Burne-Jones girl really looked like!

THE END

Acknowledgements

I must begin with my own Rotary Club, the Rotary Club of Swindon Old Town all of whose members have been so supportive. I must single out Peter Elliott for special mention. Apart from being an invaluable proof reader, he has been the person whose kind words and encouragement have kept me going and given me the confidence to get the book published but no Peter, I will not be having a DNA Test to see if I am related to Agatha Christie. I must also thank my Club's Youth Committee for their good work in promoting the Young Photographer Competition which has led to me being able to use District 1100 Intermediate Age Young Photographer for the cover pictures. I must thank Alex Milton for producing such evocative photographs for the cover photos and Anne Bartholomew District Governor for the foreword and the kind words it contains. Last but not least in the last week before going to the printers, Angela Jensen Peter Elliott put in a lot of work not only in proof reading but in doing much the professional publishers would have done in order to aid the Rotary cause

As regards inspirations for this book I would have to begin with my own Uncle and Aunt, Jack and Doreen Ray, who took me on so many holidays to Bournemouth and Sandbanks from whence a ferry trip brought me to the "Ingrained Island" that is Purbeck. It is thanks to a former member of my club and now a member of the

Swanage and Purbeck Rotary Club, Steve Parsons, who invited us to the sixtieth anniversary of that Club. This visit reawakened my interest in the area. It is the generosity of my Aunt in leaving me her entire estate that has enabled me to fund this project. The book is a work of fiction with an imaginary village set in the Island of Purbeck and peopled with imaginary people but the solid bricks and mortar of a real church provide the setting of the murder.

Much of the writing of this book, set in twentieth century rural England was done in an Italian Restaurant in the twenty first century but it provided a strangely conducive atmosphere to get my creative as well as my digestive juices flowing. The professor thanks all the staff there who make him feel so welcome and at ease. Rest assured I will find room for Luigi Riva to play alongside Don Rogers in my all-time World Greats team!

Everyone has a great teacher to thank I had many. I will single out two I was taught by and one I taught with. Mike Nettlefold, I suspect, was a man whose lessons would have been poorly graded by Ofsted but he invoked and created in me a love of history and its characters that no formulaic lesson structure could have done. Fergus O'Conner salutes you. Miss Masters was my English teacher and a lady on who I had a terrible schoolboy crush. I had been given an essay to write on the importance of staying awake in lessons by another teacher and having completed it in a way that was judged impertinent was given another on Humour. This was evidently passed to Miss Masters for I was summoned to the front of the class and complemented on what a splendid piece of writing it was and what a marvellous understanding of Shakespeare it showed. It was the proudest moment of my writing career. The teacher I taught with and wish to mention is Jeff Davies. I apologise for ruining his theory that people who loved reading were good and spelling and thank him for his advice and comments on this book and many other things I have written.

Acknowledgements

I am a distinctly Luddite when it comes to technology and I must that those who have converted a raw doc in to a correctly formatted book. In this respect Nigel Mitchell in particular and Biddles in general, have saved a lot of heartache. Last but not least my partner, Julie Burbidge. Besides contributing a lot of help in proof reading she deals with all of life's mundane problems allowing me time to wander off in to fantasy places like Lyddcastle. I am so glad our paths crossed.

Ronald Knox wrote Ten Commandments for detective fiction. You can look them up on the Internet. It has not stopped many excellent books which break them being written. What follows are my ten rules, less advice for the competition entrants than an indication of what someone who buys any future book I write as to what they can expect.

The person who dies should be old or so evil that even Mother Teresa would struggle to refrain from sticking a dagger in their guts.

Do not be too definite in describing physical characteristics. Character is more important than appearance and do not destroy someone's visualisation of a character by giving too many details of their physique, eye or hair colouring.

You can take a good book anywhere and vice verse. Descriptions of place should be evocative and take the reader to that venue.

Remember the Gilbert and Sullivan lines about "when a felon is not engaged in his employment" The fact that a person is kind to elderly relatives, likes cats, or never cheats at golf does not mean they could not be a murderer.

Make sure the level of scientific knowledge fits the period. One of the beauties of setting a fictional story of murder in the past is it takes away possibilities of DNA and the need for a deep forensic knowledge by the author.

If a thriller writer should try to keep the reader turning the pages and not put the book down in a Murder Mystery you should try to make their book like a good bottle of red wine: to be savoured and not downed in one. There is no harm if a reader is persuaded to put it down and think "who dun it"

Keep problems of detectives' private lives out of it. There are enough sad stories of illness and family conflict. I don't really want to know about the problems in the home lives of my detectives. I want to be able to concentrate on the case they are trying to solve.

The concept of what is justice should be explored and usually people should get their just deserts.

Try to make sure at least some people live happy ever after. In the nature of a book where someone is murdered and someone found to be responsible it cannot apply to all characters but try to make sure it happens to some.

People are likely to buy future books if they know they will be meeting some characters again.

BEFORE DISPOSING OF THIS BOOK

If you are **Under 25** or indeed know somebody who is under 25 have you read the following page on a writing competition and its details.

If you are a **Rotarian** and would like to raise funds for your club you can make £5 from each copy of the book sold for your club's and know that the remainder goes to other charities. If you would like to take up this offer e mail maticdick@gmail.com

If you are not a Rotarian but would like to know more about the Rotary movement and might be interested in joining then contact

RIBI   by phone on 01789 765411

By e mail via the Rotary website

Or write to The Rotary support centre at

Kinwarton Road, Alcester, Warwickshire B49 6PB

Rules of the Competition

- The story must be a "who dunnit" not necessarily a murder set in the twentieth century.
- It should not be more that 5,000 in length.
- It must be written by a person under the age of 25 on 1st January 2024
- It must be submitted before the end of May 2024

Entries should be accompanied by a copy of the entry form overleaf

Competition Entry Form

Name _____

Contact e mail or address _____

_____

_____

Entry Submitted in hard copy of by e mail_____

Title of story _____

Name of Rotary Club submitted to _____

I certify that I am under 25 years of age and that I have read and agree to abide by the rules of the competition

Signature

_____

Signature of parent or Guardian (only needed if Under 18)

_____